stolen
lies

USA TODAY BESTSELLING AUTHOR
K WEBSTER
NIKKI ASH

My life was brutal, horrific, ruthless.

Dark.

Until a beautiful bride was dragged into my life.

I took her as my prize and made her mine.

Vengeance never tasted so sweet.

I see her truths every day, and it's hard not to fall for a woman who makes me weak.

She can try to run, but I have no intention of ever letting her go.

I wanted to marry for hate, but it looks like hate is a lie.

To the brave readers who are back for more. We promise not to put *too* much strain on your heart.

stolen
lies

chapter
one

Kostas
One Year Later

LIES.

All fucking lies.

Both of the assholes lie straight to my face. I'll kill them both. An evil laugh erupts from me, making them both wince in exactly the same way at exactly the same time.

"Is that your final answer?" I ask, grinning.

"Y-Yes," the fuckface says. "M-My final answer."

The room spins and I close my eyes. Blood. Sweat. Piss. The scents emanating from this cellar have my bile rising. Fuck, I'm going to puke.

I slice through the air and miss them both. Irritated, I stomp over to the table and grab my bottle of tequila. Adrian clears his throat as I guzzle down the liquid, but I ignore him. The burn races down my esophagus and then hums through my veins.

"I hate liars," I mumble and take another swig. "You're a liar."

The man—some Galani idiot cousin whose name doesn't

even matter to me—whimpers. "Please," he begs. "Please don't kill me. I told you everything."

Ignoring his pleading, I swipe the air again. This time I get them both right across the chest. This makes me laugh. His cries of pain are fucking entertaining.

"Sir," Adrian says.

Swiveling around, the room spins, and I stumble at the movement. When everything slows to a stop, I find two Adrians too. Both scowling at me. What the fuck is his problem?

"Got something to say?" I demand, my voice a husky slur.

He shakes his head. "Nope. Just fucking hungry."

What time is it?

What fucking day is it?

Fury burns through my chest hotter than the tequila. These days, I'm losing sight of myself. My purpose. Everything.

Don't think about it.

Don't think about it.

Blond hair. Blue eyes. Pouty as fuck lips.

Pain chases away the anger and the ache inside my chest threatens to rip me in two. I grit my teeth so I don't do something stupid like throw myself onto the floor kicking and screaming like a goddamn toddler.

She's gone.

Been gone for a motherfucking year.

All leads are dead ends.

Even this slimy asshole tonight was a dead end. He knows nothing. Nothing of value. I've sliced enough of his skin that if he knew the answer, he would've given it up already. But he hasn't because he doesn't know shit.

Where are you, Talia?

Someone took her. I can feel it in my bones. But all the usual suspects are quiet and in hiding. Everything feels so normal. As if I imagined my wife—imagined holding her luscious curves and driving into her tight heat. Sometimes I wonder if I did. Was it all a fucked-up dream? Am I in some unknown level of hell?

I swing out again, missing the Galani roach and his double. Squinting, they become one. Ugly motherfucker. Him and his blurred phantom twin.

Everything turns black for a moment and I stumble. I'm just blinking away the confusion when Adrian forcefully grabs my knife.

"Let me finish up here, Boss." He pins me with a hard glare. Why the fuck does he have four eyes?

"What'd I miss?" Aris asks, clomping down the stairs. "Yuck. A fucking mess is what."

"Kostas was just heading up to grab some coffee and a bite to eat," Adrian says. "You came just in time."

Aris rakes his gaze down my form and his lips purse together in disappointment. Same fucking way Mamá's did. My heart fucking hurts. His stare softens as he grabs my arm and hooks it over his shoulders.

"Come on, bro," Aris mutters. "Let's get you back home."

My home is empty and cold. I hate it.

"Wanna swim?" I slur, leaning heavily into him.

He chuckles. "And watch your ass drown? Maybe later."

"Let me guess," I grumble. "You gotta get home to your wife."

A snort escapes him. "Selene is not my wife."

"Yet."

"Yet," he concedes. "But she sure as fuck acts like one, always bitching if I don't get home at a decent hour."

I laugh. "At least you get laid."

"If I get home in time," he jokes.

We stumble up the stairs and he helps me into his Porsche. The drive back to my villa makes me nauseous. I'm about to puke when the car finally comes to a stop. He helps me out of the car and into my villa. I groan when I scent lemons. The maid's been by, which means she had to clean up after my latest rage. Everything has been replaced and put back together again. I fist my hands, eager to destroy it once more.

"Dude," Aris groans. "You have got to quit trashing your villa. Do you know how much money we've spent on fixing this room? I thought we were past this."

I'll never be past this.

Talia.

Just fucking gone.

"She's dead," I tell him, my words choking my throat.

He sighs. "You don't know that."

"She is."

With a grunt, he drops me onto my sofa. I fade in and out of consciousness as I hear the microwave beeping. Something savory makes my stomach grumble. Aris sets down a plate of microwaved pizza on the coffee table.

"Eat, man. You're wasting away."

I shrug. "I'm not hungry."

He crosses his arms over his chest and levels me with a serious glare. I roll my eyes as I take a bite of the pizza. My, how our roles have reversed. I think Aris secretly likes taking care of me as I wallow in my fucking misery. I'd say he gets off on it, but his concerned eyes that are exactly like Mamá's don't lie. And because of that, I eat the damn pizza.

"I really do need to bail," he mutters. "I hate leaving you like this, but Selene can be such a bitch."

"Married life," I say with a grunt.

"Not yet." He laughs. "Hell, maybe not ever."

"You bought a fucking house for her." I scratch at my jaw. "Am I an embarrassment?"

"Truly, you are," he taunts, his brown eyes lighting up with playfulness.

"Fuck off. You never have me over."

"You've been preoccupied. You think I want to rub in your face the fact I'm happy with Selene and thinking about popping the question while you're dying over here in despair? Hell no. I may think you're a dick, but I'm not going to do that shit to you."

I chew the pizza and frown before swallowing it. "Don't tell me you let her decorate."

He winces. "The kitchen is seashell themed."

"Jesus," I say with a laugh. "Mamá would be rolling over in her grave."

We both sober up momentarily.

"I miss her," Aris rumbles. "I miss her so fucking much."

I, however, have mixed feelings on the matter. She fucked over my dad. Sure, he can be a dick. Like me. But did he deserve to be cheated on for a damn decade? Did he deserve to be shot because he was angry about the affair? He sure as hell didn't deserve to lose his ability to walk because she couldn't keep from having sex with Niles Fucking Nikolaides.

Is that what happened to Talia? Did she run off with her secret lover?

No one fucking knows. Especially not me.

"Maybe when you're not getting fucked up, you can come over for dinner one day. Make some décor suggestions to Selene."

"Maybe," I grumble. We both know I'm not leaving this fucking hotel to go give interior decorating advice to my brother's whore wannabe wife.

Aris leaves the room and returns shortly with a glass of ouzo. He smiles as he sets it down next to the plate. "My peace offering."

"Who knew you could be so cordial, brother?"

He grins. "Someone has to take care of your broody ass."

I suck down the ouzo and then slam the glass back down on the table. "You out?"

"Yeah. I'm out. See you tomorrow."

"Any leads?"

A frown mars his features. "If I had any, you'd be the first to know." He lets out a heavy sigh. "We'll find her, Kostas."

Bones in a ditch.

Hair hanging from a vat of acid.

Her big diamond ring at the bottom of the sea.

That's how I imagine we'll find her one day.

I hate that I'm losing faith we'll find her alive. It's been so long. Her mother is devastated. Phoenix is damn near crazed. And me, I'm fucking destroyed.

A year.

A motherfucking year.

It's not getting better. It's getting much, much worse.

"If you want me to stay with you and talk," Aris says, "I can tell Selene we're working more leads. I don't like that look in your eyes." He clenches his jaw. "You can't do to me what Mamá did to us. Don't leave me with our damn dad all alone."

6

He thinks I'm going to kill myself.

It's like he doesn't know me at all.

I don't want to kill myself…

I want to kill anyone and everyone involved in the disappearance of my wife.

And if Talia left me of her own accord, well, I'll deal with her ass when I find her.

"Go," I grunt. "Go play house."

He smirks. "You're jealous."

"Jealous you're going to get your dick sucked? Fuck yes. But by Selene? Hell no. Sorry, Aris, but she's a snotty bitch."

Rather than be offended, he shrugs. "She gives good head."

We both laugh and then he lets out a sigh.

"One more peace offering and then I'm gone," he grunts. "You can get your lazy ass up off your couch if you want any more. Tomorrow, come to the office sober and we can shake up some more leads."

He disappears and once again returns with my glass refilled with ouzo. With a tip of his head, he leaves me with my alcohol and my depressing thoughts. After I suck down the drink, I stumble into the bathroom, shedding my bloody clothes along the way. I take a long, hot shower and lean my head against the cool tile. My hand rubs at my dick, but between the ouzo and my shitty attitude, it's not interested in release.

"What the fuck ever," I grunt out.

Once I'm dry, I wrap my towel around my waist and fall onto the bed. I reach into the drawer, pulling out my iPad. Turning it on, I open the pictures app and find ones I have saved of Talia.

In the photos, her blue eyes are alight with fire. She was

so alive. She loved to challenge me. I loved it right back. Loved her.

Now?

I still fucking love her, which is why this shit hurts so bad. I let her leave that day pissed at me when I should have dragged her back to bed to leave love notes with my mouth all over her body. I should have spoken those words. Maybe it could have made a difference. Maybe she would still be here with me.

Scrolling past several pictures, I find my favorite. One of her lying in bed, her hair messy and her tits exposed. They're red from my mouth and her nipples are hard. The sultry look on her face just begs me to come back to bed and fuck her again. Again and again and again. That's not the look of someone who'd willingly leave. Deep down, I feel that in my heart. But my head? My head wonders if she was acting all along.

Refusing to think badly about her when all I want is to fucking come, I undo my towel and fist my cock that's come to life upon seeing her picture. She's still my wife. Until I know she's dead or left me, I'll go on the assumption she's alive somewhere out there missing me. I stroke and stroke, fixating on her plump lips. Her full tits. Her hooded eyes. Closing my eyes, I remember back to how tight she felt when I'd push into her slick cunt. How her tits would jiggle and she'd moan so fucking sweetly. Her fingernails would scrape down my shoulders and she'd beg for release. I groan when my nuts seize up. Heat splatters on my stomach and my chest heaves. When I reopen my eyes, I realize I've accidentally slid to the next picture. It's one of her at the opening of Pomegranate that her mother took. I stole it from her mom's social media like a fucking creepy stalker.

God, she's beautiful.

She's still out there.

She has to be.

As my eyes droop, I silently make a vow.

I'm coming for you, moró mou. *I'm always coming for you.*

And one day I'm going to find you.

chapter
two

Talia

“I N THE UNDERWORLD, PROSERPINA HAS GROWN TO love Pluto, who treated her with compassion and loved her as his Queen. As she would have up in Olympus, she remained eternally beautiful in the Underworld. Pluto admired her kind and nurturing nature. However, Proserpina missed her dear mother greatly and wished to spend time on earth with her. When Hermes reached the underworld, he requested that Proserpina come back to earth with him to rejoin her mother and father.” I turn the page of the book, and a tiny hand swats out at the page, wrinkling it slightly.

“No, no, sweet girl,” I tell her gently. “We have to be nice to the book.” She looks up at me with her radiant bright blue eyes and giggles, and my heart feels as though it’s thumped straight out of my chest. But I guess that comes with the territory. My mom used to always tell me being a mom means removing your heart and giving it to your children.

Wiping a drop of liquid emotion from my cheek, I continue to read my favorite part of the book. “Pluto knew he could not refuse the commands of Zeus, but he also could not part from his beloved Proserpina." A golf ball sized lump fills my throat, and I have to set the book down for a minute to gather myself together. It always happens when I get to this part. Thoughts of *him* surface and I have to force them away. It's the only way.

With a deep breath, I continue to read the story. "Before she departed from the underworld, Pluto offered Proserpina a pomegranate as a farewell. This was, however, a cunning move by Pluto. All the Olympians knew that if anyone ate or drank anything in the Underworld they would be destined to remain there for—"

"That book again?" a shrill voice, equivalent to nails grinding on a chalkboard, says, ruining story time.

Without turning to face the owner of the voice, I close the book and stare out at the blue waters of Mirabello Bay. From up here, I can't smell the salt water, but I can still see the waves lapping up at the shore, and sometimes when I close my eyes, I can imagine being down there, lying in a hammock, smelling the scent of—

"You know it doesn't understand anything you're saying, right?" the annoying voice continues, snapping me out of my daydream. "It's a baby," she snarls.

"And that's why I'm the mom and you're the maid." I give my daughter a kiss on her forehead and inhale her fresh baby scent that's mixed with chlorine from our swim in the pool earlier. "*She's* not an *it*. And she's almost six months old. She's sitting up and crawling. She laughs and…" I turn around to face *the maid*, annoyed at myself for allowing her to work me up, but I can't help it. Every time she speaks of my daughter as if she's some alien, it riles up my mama bear instincts and I pounce.

11

When my eyes scan down her body, I notice she's dressed in a skimpy shrimp-colored dress and white heels, her face full of makeup, like she's about to go to the club instead of rotate the laundry. Her collagen-filled lips are pursed together in a mixture of hate and confusion, and I roll my eyes. I don't know why I even bother to try to explain anything to her. She doesn't have a single maternal bone in her body. I pity anything—plant, human, animal, mineral—she attempts to care for. It will be dead within days.

I shake my head, giving up on explaining to her for the millionth time, my daughter is probably smarter at six months old than she is at…however old she is. It's hard to tell. Her voice is screechy and whiny, giving off a young vibe, but all the makeup makes her appear to be older. "Never mind. What do you want?"

"Dinner's ready." Oh, dear Lord, please tell me she's ordered something. If I have to eat one more of her home-cooked meals I'm going to throw myself off this cliff. I'm going to seriously have to have a talk with Aris when he gets home. Just because she's decided she wants to try and play house, doesn't mean I have to be punished.

"I'm not hungry. I'll eat later." I open the book to read more of the story to my sweet girl.

"I wasn't asking," she informs me. "I was telling you. Aris brought dinner home and he's waiting." She rolls her eyes, obviously annoyed that the man she's in love with doesn't feel the same and would rather have my company than hers.

"Fine," I snap. "I'll be there in a few minutes."

She turns on her heel to head back up to the house, when I call her name. "Oh, and *Selene*, my daughter would like her sweet potatoes pureed with only a *hint* of butter. The last time you made them there was enough butter in them to give a grown man a heart attack."

She huffs, but doesn't argue. *Damn right, bitch, know your place.*

"You ready to eat dinner, sweet girl?" I coo at my daughter, who throws her chubby little arms in the air and giggles. It's the most beautiful, melodic sound in the world.

After taking one last look down below, I stand and carry her into the mansion of a house. With at least ten bedrooms, and even more bathrooms, it would take a map to find your way around the entire place. But lucky for me, the only room I need to be able to find is my daughter's, which is on the first floor attached to mine. I give her a quick bath to get the chlorine off her body and then feed her a bottle. When I'm done, I head to the dining room.

"Nice of you to finally join me, dear." Aris stands and makes his way over to my daughter and me.

"I had to feed her first," I explain. "But I'm here now."

"And how is my daughter?" Aris asks, taking her from me before I can stop him.

"*Zoe* is perfect," I tell him, opening the lid to her high chair, so he can set her in it. "Selene!" I call out. "I need Zoe's dinner now!"

Aris chuckles, but doesn't say a word. He never does. The only reason why he keeps her around is because he knows how obsessed the woman is with him, which means she'll do anything he asks of her.

"And how was your day?" Aris asks after pulling my chair out for me and then sitting at the head of the table. Selene saunters into the dining room, her heels *click-clacking* against the marble floor. She drops Zoe's sweet potatoes down in front of me and they spill out of the cup. They look overcooked and gross. Good thing I never planned to feed these to her.

"Actually," I tell her, stifling my smile, "she's not that hungry. She just had a bottle." I reach over and grab Zoe's container of fruit and place some on her tray. "You can take this away." I lift the bowl of sweet potatoes and wait for her to take them. Which she does. Because she's the maid.

I begin eating my chicken and realize it's from Pomegranate, the restaurant I built from the ground up. Aris is probably hoping for a reaction, but he's not going to get one.

"I asked how your day was," Aris repeats.

"Fine."

"Just fine?" he prompts.

"That's what I said."

Selene sits at the table across from me, on the other side of Aris. "My back hurts," she complains. "I swear that baby accumulates so much laundry. Can we please hire someone?"

"That's what we have you for," Aris snaps, and I snort out a laugh.

"But, Aris…" she whines.

"No buts," he tells her, shutting down the conversation.

After dinner is over, I grab one of the cupcakes from the pantry I made for today. Snagging a lighter and candle from the drawer, I take everything with me onto the veranda. When I go back inside to grab Zoe, Aris has her in his arms. It's not often he holds her…

"Can I have her, please?" I extend my arms to grab her and she shifts her body toward me. *That's my girl…*

Aris doesn't hand her to me, but instead walks outside. "A cupcake?" he asks, even though he knows the drill.

"She's six months old today." Closing my eyes so the tears that are burning my lids don't fall, I take in a deep, cleansing breath. But when I open my eyes, a couple traitor tears fall. Aris, of course, mistakes them for me being a sentimental mother.

"Don't be sad, Talia. Growing up is inevitable."

"Can I borrow your phone to take a picture?" I ask. Aris chuckles.

"How about you hold her and I'll take the picture?" He hands me back Zoe.

I light the candle and Aris snaps a picture of the two of us before I blow it out and make a wish. A wish... Every birthday when I was growing up my mom would tell me to make a wish using the candles on the cake. I used to wish for trite things like a new bike, the bracelet I wanted. For my mom to let me go to the movies with my friends. Now, though, even though they're technically Zoe's wishes, every time I blow out the candle for her, I make the same wish. For—

"Talia," Aris says, breaking me from my thought. "Selene is going into town with me tomorrow. Make sure you make a list of anything you need."

My eyes snap to Aris's, but I quickly school my features, not wanting him to have any clue what I'm thinking.

"I'll make a list. And can you please have that picture printed for me?" I point to his phone, holding the picture of Zoe and me.

"Of course. Anything for you." He pulls me into his side and kisses my temple. "Anything for you."

chapter
three

Kostas

MY HEAD THROBS LIKE A MOTHERFUCKER. There was a time, when Talia disappeared, that I was clearheaded and hell-bent on finding her. I exhausted every resource I had into looking into what happened. Nothing ever came of it, though. She just fucking vanished.

Just like Michael and Tadd.

I remember torturing those incompetent fools because someone had to pay. It was their job to protect her. They had one fucking job and they failed. Adrian and Basil brought them in, strapped them to chairs, and handed me weapon after weapon until I drained them of every ounce of life.

It didn't make her reappear. She was still gone.

Leaning back in my office chair, I ignore my phone as it buzzes. Another call from my father. It drives him insane that he's stuck at his house in forced retirement. Aris and I visit him to share meals on occasion, but whenever he tries to talk business, we shut him down. I can thank my brother for that much—having my back against our father. Father is out of touch. It's Aris and I who deal with the business day in and day out. In fact, now that I've given Aris more responsibility in the past year, we've thrived. Money just fucking floods in.

Unfortunately, I don't give a shit about money.

I'm obsessed with finding Talia.

For the millionth time, I wonder about Alex. The scuzzy American fucker she dated before she came to be my wife. I know everything about the asshole. His flavor of the week. His favorite restaurant. His shitty taste in music. I follow him on every social media outlet because I figure one day he's going to slip up. One day I'll learn he has her hidden away while they play house together, laughing at the fact I'm finally out of the picture. In those dark fantasies, I slaughter Alex and make Talia watch. Then, I fuck her back into submission. It's easier being angry with her. At least there's hope threaded in with my anger. Hope that she's alive and I'll find her one day. It's a helluva lot better than the alternative: her being dead.

My eyes drag from my phone over to the bottle of ouzo sitting on my desk. I practically shake with the need to drink. I'm not stupid. I'm well aware of the fact I'm drinking myself into oblivion. And the more I drink, the further from finding her I feel. But when it's staring me in the face, it's hard to push it away. At least when I'm drinking, my body goes numb. The bleeding in my fucking heart stops.

Ignoring the ouzo, I grab my phone and pull up Alex's Instagram. He's back in Florence with a brunette tucked under his arm. His eyes are hooded as he smiles crookedly at the camera. It boils my blood that Talia was once with this idiot. I've often thought about dragging him here to my hotel so I could cut off every part of his body that may have once touched her. Adrian's eyes grew wide at my suggestion, which is the only reason I didn't follow through. I know Adrian looks out for me and with one wild expression, I knew I was acting like a madman and not like the cunning mobster I am.

But so help me if that fucker Alex has Talia or knows where she's at…

I scrub my hand down my face and begin scrolling through my contacts. I find Talia's mother, Melody, and stare at her name. This woman used to hate me, but now we share a common goal: find Talia. Melody wears her heart on her sleeve when it comes to her daughter. If she were hiding her or knew where she was, I'd know about it. I put the phone on speaker and dial her. She answers on the first ring.

"Kostas," she greets, her voice tight with concern. "Any word?"

She always answers right away, hopeful I've found Talia.

"No," I grunt out. "Any news on your end?"

A heavy sigh escapes her. "None."

We share a long moment of silence, both of us brooding.

"Emilio hasn't heard any chatter?" I'm always hopeful with his governmental position and contacts with the police, he might hear of some organization somewhere bragging over the fact they got Kostas Demetriou's wife.

"Nothing," she says. "I spoke with him today and nothing. Niles?"

I wince at his name. "Still missing also."

Another long moment of silence. It's a theory we've discussed before. Niles taking her and hiding her away. The motive is unclear, but it's one that makes a lot of sense. She is his daughter and he hates our family. It could be a way to stick it to us. He's just not smart enough or rich enough for that shit. It doesn't add up.

"I will be visiting Phoenix soon," I tell her. "I'll see what I can find out."

"Don't hurt my son."

I smirk. She's like Talia in that sense. Bossing around a crime lord like it's not a big fucking deal. But, because it reminds me of her daughter, I give her allowances I shouldn't. "We'll see."

She must not hear any threat in my words because she lets out a relieved sigh. "What about on Crete? My father said not long before she was taken, Ezio had an attempt on his life by the Galanis. Could they be behind this?"

It irritates me she knows so much about our world, but again, she's her daughter's mother. I can't fault her for being dedicated to plucking up every stone to see if it leads to her daughter. I'll take all the help I can get at this point.

"Most of the Galanis are gone," I bite out. "The dickless one is still out and about, but he doesn't have the spine to do something grand like kidnap my wife. Plus, he'd love to gloat. If he had her, he'd torment me with that fact. Since everything is silent, it tells me it's someone new or someone who couldn't care less about taunting me, but maybe someone with their own agendas."

"She's such a beautiful woman," her mother breathes. "What if someone kidnapped her and sold her into a sex trafficking ring? Do you know people who do that sort of thing?"

No, but your ex-husband does.

"I doubt that's it." I fucking hope that's not it. "But to be safe, I'll bring it up to Phoenix at our meeting. Niles admitted to allowing passage with some new clients who were into that shit."

She lets out a ragged breath. "Kostas, we have to find her. If she's with sex traffickers…" A loud sob escapes her. "I worry we'll never get the Talia we know and love back."

I scrub my face in frustration. "Whoever has her will fucking pay," I growl. "I will skin them all alive."

My words don't frighten her. "Good. They deserve it for taking my baby girl."

Voices echo down the hallway just outside my office and I sit up straight. "I need to go."

"Okay, *cara mio*, take care and let me know if you learn anything new."

I hang up and let her words sink in. Lately, she calls me *her darling* like I really am her son. And fuck if I don't correct her because it makes me miss Mamá.

Frustration churns in my gut. I rise from my chair and stalk outside onto the veranda. This afternoon, the air is warm and the salty sea scent evokes memories of my honeymoon. Taking Talia on the beach for the first time. The look of pure adoration on her pretty face as I made her mine. It's times like these, when I'm sobering up, everything feels so crystal clear. I think back to that week when we located Estevan Galani in that apartment building. How he'd eyed up my wife like she was trash he wanted to burn. The fact he survived his injuries I gave him wasn't surprising, but the fact he remains in hiding and not fucking with me is a disturbing fact. It feels important. Like I need to pursue why he isn't fucking with me. I shot his dick off, for fuck's sake. If someone shot my dick off, I'd try to destroy them, and would die doing it too.

Think, Kostas.

My mind wanders to the day she disappeared. We fought like fucking hell, but it wasn't a relationship ending fight. Too many times I've allowed myself to blame it on that. That she was pissed and finally left me. She'd met up with Selene and asked for money. Another big mystery.

I'd assumed she took the money and used it to get away.

But what if she was being blackmailed?

Rushing back inside, I sit at my desk and unlock my computer. When she went missing, I made sure the backups of our security footage were being stored in another place. I've scoured through tons of it, but often, I get frustrated sifting through hours and hours of footage that leads to nothing. The footage that never made sense was the night she supposedly took the money from Selene. I want to view it again. I pull back the footage to that night and find where we last enter the villa. Then, I skim through the night, waiting for her to leave. It eventually skips to the next day when she storms out to leave for school. I check all the cameras surrounding the villa, and nothing shows up.

Selene claimed Talia borrowed money from her, but it didn't happen that night.

She never left.

Which means either Selene confused the events or lied to me.

Why?

I assess Selene's behavior over the past year. She's obsessed with Aris. I bet she was even jealous of Talia, even though Talia was my woman and not Aris's. Would she lie to us to make Talia seem like a bad person who left me? And why?

She's a catty cunt, but she's not smart enough to pull off

some grand kidnapping of my wife and keep it from me all this time. Most likely she just wanted to make Talia look bad. Regardless, I'm going to find out why the fuck Selene would lie because it doesn't help me get to the bottom of this shit with her meddling.

"Frown any harder and your face may stick that way," a familiar voice booms from the doorway.

As soon as I see my brother, I click out of the video footage and pop open Google on my browser before turning to him. "This is my face. It's been stuck this way since I turned thirteen."

He snorts. "I can't believe Dad actually gave us lessons on how to look fierce and intimidating."

"You failed," I grunt out.

"And you passed with flying colors. But seriously? What kind of father teaches their kids that?"

I shrug and glance at the clock, before watching every tick of my brother's face. "Want to have dinner?"

His brown eyes flash for a second before he schools his features, not taking my bait. "Of course."

"Actually," I mutter. "I need to get ready for my trip to Thessaloniki."

Aris's shoulders relax slightly. "Raincheck then. We could always go visit Dad and have dinner with him."

It's sad how much he desperately tries to gain Father's favor. Even now. Even with Father being practically an invalid and meaner than a snake. My mother's death killed him more than he'll ever let on.

"Sure," I tell him with a shrug.

"Anything new?" He walks over to the wet bar in my office and pulls out two tumblers. After he fills them with ice and a little water, he heads back over to my desk. I'm silent as I watch him fill them with ouzo. He pushes a glass my way and then he proceeds to sip his.

Not touching the glass, I cross my arms over my chest and lean back in my chair. "Nothing."

His lips purse together. "We'll come up with something eventually."

My stare on him must unnerve him because he waves a hand at the ouzo. "Drink up, man. I have to get home to Selene soon or I'll never hear the end of it."

"Sure are pussy-whipped," I say, picking up the glass and swirling the ice around in it.

He snorts. "She knows her place."

"Where is Estevan Galani?" I ask, setting my tumbler down.

His eyebrows hike in surprise at my question and then he gives me a one-shouldered shrug. "Your guess is as good as mine. Went silent after you blew his cock off."

I scrub at the scruff on my face. "Galanis aren't known for their silence. They have the biggest goddamn mouths on Crete."

His lips press into a thin line. A worried line. It makes me scrutinize him further. "I'll look into it."

"Good," I grunt. "So will I."

"Cheers to dealing with the Galani infestation," he says, raising his glass and imploring me to drink.

I rise from my seat and walk over to the door. "I'll never toast to a fucking Galani. Go on and get out of here before your viper girlfriend tries to make a meal out of your balls."

He drains his glass and slams it down with a hard clunk. Then, he stands, shooting me an unreadable expression. With a deep breath, he inhales and then exhales whatever was threatening his composure. A wide grin spreads across his face.

"Have a good night, Kostas," he says with a smug grin. "My night will be a helluva lot better than yours, I can assure you."

He walks out without another word.

I glance over at my untouched ouzo and straighten my spine. I've been a cloud for far too long.

It's time to wake the fuck up and find my goddamn wife.

chapter
four

Talia

"I NEED MORE FORMULA," I YELL OVER THE SCREAMS of my pissed off daughter.

Selene glares my way. "I was just in town a few days ago. Aris told you to make a list." She eyes me accusingly, but I just shrug nonchalantly, not bothering to settle Zoe down. Her screaming always flusters Selene. For the sake of the human population, the woman should be sterilized so she can never reproduce.

"I did make a list." Zoe's screams get louder. "But Zoe had a growth spurt and I ran out sooner than I expected. Babies grow," I challenge.

"And you don't have any left at all?" she questions. I can see it in her features, she's about to reach her limit. Her hands are shaking, and her eyes are twitching. Come on, bitch…

"If I did I wouldn't be asking. Look, if you don't want to go, I can." I shrug with a smirk that I know will piss her off. "Zoe isn't going to stop crying until she's fed." As if on cue, Zoe's screams get louder. Every wail from her squeezes my heartstrings, but it's for the greater good.

"Jesus!" Selene shouts over the loud crying. "Fine. I'm going." She knows damn well she'll be in trouble if my daughter is unhappy in any way. A pissed off Zoe leads to a pissed off Aris. And a pissed off Aris never ends well. We've both learned that the hard way. The only difference is Aris actually cares about me since I'm the mother of his daughter, whereas with Selene, he views her as nothing more than a human pincushion. Poking every hole when he feels like it. The thought has me gagging. Better her than me, though.

Frustrated, she quickly unlocks the key box right in front of me, just as I hoped she would. Seven-two-two-four. She grabs a set of keys, slams it closed, then heads over to the garage door. I watch as she types in the code. Four-nine-nine-five. The light flashes green and she opens then closes the door behind her. I wait until I hear the garage door open and close and then I run into the kitchen. I type in the code to the key box and it clicks open. Grabbing the pair of keys, I pull one off the ring and put the other one back. As I'm closing the box, I spot Selene's cell phone on the counter. Holy shit! She forgot her phone.

Grabbing it, I tap the screen. It comes to life, but there's a password. No problem since I know it. Four-six-three-six. I type it in, but it's wrong. What the hell! I type it in again, but it's still wrong. I saw her type it in myself. This has to be right. The phone prompts I only have one try left before it locks.

I hear the garage opening back up. Damn it! She must've realized she forgot her phone. What do I do? Then it hits me. I bring up the passcode screen and hit the emergency button. The car door slams closed as the call connects.

"What is your emergency?"

I run with the phone in one hand and Zoe in the other

to hide in another room. "My name is Talia Demetriou and I need you to—"

Before I can finish my sentence, my head is yanked back and the phone is snatched from my hand. "You bitch!" Selene yells. She raises her hand to slap me, but I duck. Zoe is now screaming bloody murder, and I'm running to get away from Selene so she doesn't inadvertently hurt my daughter. I make it into Zoe's room and slam the door just before Selene can touch either of us.

The door doesn't lock, so with my weight against the door, I grab the rocking chair and wedge it under the doorknob so Selene can't get in. Once I know we're safe, I make Zoe a bottle and feed it to her. She calms down right away, and once she's full, falls asleep in my arms.

Since there's no way I'm going back out there until Aris gets home, I use the time to go over my list. Stealing Selene's cell phone wasn't my original plan anyway. I just saw it on the counter and figured it was worth a try. Pulling the small diaper bag out from under my bed, I double-check everything I've accumulated over the last several months. Formula, bottles, diapers, wipes, clothes for Zoe and me, three knives, over two hundred euros. Reaching into my pocket, I add the spare keys I stole to Aris's SUV. Selene and Aris will be so focused on me trying to steal her phone, they won't even think about the fact my entire purpose was to steal his keys.

Not wanting to risk the bag being seen, I shove it back under the bed. While Zoe naps, I read a book, and once she wakes up, I spend the rest of the day playing with her in her room. It isn't until I hear Aris's voice on the other side of the door, I move the chair and open the door.

"I heard you've been busy today," he says, eyeing me with annoyance.

"I was scared for my life," I cry out. "Selene is psycho, Aris. The only reason I tried to call the police was because I was scared." Tears prick my eyes, but Aris just rolls his.

"Stop your shit, Talia. Your little stunt today was stupid on your part." Aris smirks. "Want to know why?" I don't bother to answer. I know he'll tell me. "Since I now have to worry about you trying shit, I had to give Selene a gun." Jesus fucking Christ. Is he serious?

"If you try anything, she's been told not to hesitate." Aris steps forward and grabs ahold of my ponytail, jerking my head up to look him in the eyes. "I don't give a shit if you live or die, Talia," he hisses. "The only reason I keep you around is so you can take care of Zoe. You're her mother and I didn't want to take you from her. But if you're going to become a problem…" He lets his sentence linger, releasing my hair. "Now, dinner is ready. Let's try to have a good night. I've had a long day at work. My brother has become a raging alcoholic and I'm now having to do both of our jobs." Aris rolls his eyes then walks out of the room.

Kostas has become an alcoholic… My heart squeezes in my chest at the thought of what he's been going through this last year. It's hard to believe anything that comes out of Aris's mouth. I knew the night he raped me, he was a wolf in sheep's clothing, but I had no idea just how deadly of a bite he had until the day I was taken.

I'm sitting in the auditorium, waiting for rehearsal to begin. I've only been here for a few minutes, but I want to go home. When I left this morning, Kostas and I were fighting. I know part of it is my fault. I'm overemotional and haven't told him why yet. Mostly because I'm scared of how he's going to react. But it's also his fault because he's so damn jealous. I have to kiss Macbeth in the play and I know Kostas is going to kill him if I do, which means I'm going to have to either tell my professor I can't play the role as Lady Macbeth or figure out a way to fake-kiss my partner, so my husband doesn't rip his heart from his chest. I want to be mad at him for being such a possessive asshole, but then he sends me a sweet text and I turn into a pile of mush.

Kostas: I miss you even when you piss me the fuck off.

Okay, well, sweet for Kostas... It's crazy to think how quickly he's become my entire world, and not because I was forced to marry him, but because I love him. The problem is, while I'm not sure if Kostas loves me back, I do know he wants to own and possess every part of me. At this rate, there is going to be no me without Kostas, and I'm scared of what will happen when I can't put him first. When I can't give him all of me. Will he still want me? Will what I can give him be enough? Or will he do what my father did and stray? The thought has me wanting to throw up.

"You are going to make the craziest Lady Macbeth," *Penelope says, sitting next to me. When I glance up at her, she frowns.* "What's wrong?"

"Nothing." *I shake my head.* "I'm okay."

"No, you're not," *she insists.* "You're crying." *She reaches over and swipes a tear off my cheek I didn't realize was there.* "Talk to me."

As if the dam that was holding back my flood of emotions caves, I let out every thought and feeling without holding back. Penelope wraps her arms around me and listens as I pour my heart out to her. She doesn't say anything the entire time as I tell her about everything I'm feeling and how much I miss my home and my family, especially my mom. When I'm done, she hugs me tightly.

"What is it that will make you okay right now?" *she asks.*

After a moment of thinking about her question, I say, "I-I think..." I hiccup through my sobs. "I think I really just want my mom." We both break out into a fit of giggles at how much of a child I sound like in this moment.

"Moms do make everything better," Penelope agrees.

I stand and wipe the tears from my face. "I'm going to go use the restroom and wash my face. Thank you for listening. Honestly, I think I just needed a good cry." I choke out another laugh and Penelope joins in.

Grabbing my purse, I throw my phone into it and walk through the side stage doors that lead to the bathroom. Setting my purse down on the sink, I wet a paper towel and wipe under my eyes until I no longer look like a raccoon.

Leaving my purse on the sink, I head into the first stall to go pee. I hear the bathroom door open and then a masculine voice yells, "Talia! You in here?" Aris? What the hell is he doing in here?

I swing open the door and find him standing in front of the door.

"We need to go now."

"What? Why?" I'm so confused.

He grabs my arm and yanks me from the stall and out of the bathroom. "I'll explain once we're in the car. Kostas sent me to get you. There's been a threat and he needs to know you're safe."

"What about Michael and Tadd?" My head is spinning.

"They are the threat," Aris says as he opens the side door to the building. Something isn't right here.

"Aris, wait!" I shout, but he doesn't listen. I reach for my phone and realize it's still in my purse...in the bathroom. Shit! "Aris, I want to speak to Kostas," I demand, but he ignores me. When I dig my feet into the grass, refusing to walk, he turns around and whips a gun out.

"Get in the fucking car, Talia," he says.

Instantly, my hands go to my stomach, fearful not only for myself, but for my baby. "Okay," I tell him. "Okay, just please don't shoot me."

The entire drive, my only thoughts are that there's a good chance I'll never see or speak to Kostas again. My last words to him were said in anger. He texted me to tell me he misses me, but I never texted him back. He'll never know how much I love him, and that I'm pregnant.

chapter
five

Kostas

THE ENTIRE THREE-HOUR FLIGHT FROM HERAKLION to Thessaloniki was difficult. Being trapped in my private plane with nothing but a stocked bar and a building rage, I was about to explode. I wanted to drown out my thoughts, but something keeps niggling at me—something I need to keep a clear head for. Like the answer is right in front of me, but I can't seem to put my finger on it.

Aris.

I want to say Aris has something to do with it, but he's afraid of me. Deep down, I know he is. Where he might willingly sleep with my wife just to show he could, he'd never kill her. And hide her away for a year, that's just bullshit Aris couldn't keep from me. I see him every day, all day. If he was hiding something huge about Talia, I'd know.

Wouldn't I?

When she was taken, I was blinded by determination to find her. Then, anger that I hadn't. Now, drowning in grief also known as fucking alcohol. Alcohol that Aris has no qualms about offering me anytime he's around.

Which is exactly why I need to keep a clear head. For the first time since she's been gone, I feel alert and aware. I didn't get to where I am today for being a blind fool.

I'm brooding on my thoughts while we hit the tarmac. The staff on the plane is accommodating, but I'm distracted by Talia. Always Talia. Once I step out of the plane, I'm irritated to see Phoenix leaned against a door-less Jeep. He's dressed casually in a pair of jeans and a black T-shirt showcasing all his tattoos and looking like a fucking escaped convict. I hate how much he looks like Talia. It's a painful reminder of my loss of her.

"Where's my car?" I grumble.

Phoenix shrugs and hops inside. I follow suit and climb into his metal death wish. I'm sure I look out of place in my Armani suit.

"Where are your men?" he asks, nodding at the plane.

"Where are yours?" I challenge back.

"I don't need them," he sneers, side-eyeing me like I'm a minnow he can easily scare away.

"Same," I bite back like the shark I am.

He smirks as he throws the Jeep into drive. We haul ass down the road into the city. It's been a while since I've come to meet him about the taxes. In the beginning I did, right after he took over for Niles, but then, when I was losing my ever-loving mind over Talia, Aris took care of business.

"Where are we going?" I demand upon realizing we're not headed toward the city where his office is.

"We can do business anywhere with our phones," he grunts out. "I'm hungry and I figured you are too."

It's noon and I didn't touch the refreshments on the flight. He's right, but I won't tell him that. He takes us to a small restaurant outside of the city. It has horrible curbside appeal, but the moment we exit the Jeep and I get a whiff of the savory garlic scents in the air, I know looks will be deceiving.

He greets the man up front and then ushers us to a dark corner booth. When he orders ouzo for the both of us, I change my order to water, which gets a lifted brow of surprise from him.

"Got a problem?"

His nostrils flare. "Nope."

As soon as the waiter runs off to fetch our drinks, Phoenix crosses his arms over his bulky chest and glowers at me.

"What?" I demand.

"Nothing," he sneers. "Just finally looking at the man who let my sister get taken. The same man who can't find her." He's pissed and his jaw muscle keeps flexing. If I had any thought that he'd taken her, it's squashed in this moment.

"You're looking at the man who will cut your throat for fucking disrespecting him," I growl, cracking my neck. "Watch your tongue, Nikolaides. Seems you forgot who you were talking to."

He grinds his teeth but relaxes his posture. "I just don't see how after all this time you haven't found her." His eyes narrow. "Unless you don't want her to be found."

"Me?" I snap. "If I wanted to get rid of her, I would have, and I'd gladly fucking tell you. I don't play little girl games."

"Then where the fuck is she?" he bellows, leaning forward, fire gleaming in his eyes. "Where the fuck is my sister?"

"Maybe she's with your father," I bite out. "Since you

can't find him and all. Maybe they're in the same magical hidden realm of the earth."

"What are you, a fuckin' fairy?" He shakes his head in frustration. "Dad is quiet, but if he had her, I'd know about it. For one, she'd drive him insane. He'd make me deal with her. Dad and Talia haven't gotten along in some time. I'm the peacemaker between the two."

The waiter brings our drinks and we order from the menu.

"What about those men who were supposed to be guarding her?" he asks bitterly. "Could they be in on it?"

I crack my knuckles before picking up my water and chugging it down. With a slam of the glass on the table, I level him with a hard glare. "We can't exactly ask them because I skinned them alive."

His brows furrow, but his eyes flash in appreciation. "Mom keeps yapping at me about the Galanis. You two chat an awful lot."

Fucking Melody.

"I want answers," I grit out.

"And Mom has them?" he challenges.

"Fuck no, she doesn't have them."

"Then why do you call her?"

Because she reminds me that Talia was a good woman who wouldn't just leave me.

"I check every lead." I lift my chin and meet his glare. "Can I say the same for you? What about the traffickers your dad was letting come through?"

"That shit ended when I took over. And I look for her every damn day, Kostas. I think that's the only fucking thing we have in common. Well, that and the inability to find her." He lets out a heavy sigh. "We'll find her."

I hate that we have a common goal. Nikolaides and Demetrious working together. It's a shitshow, clearly.

"*I'll* find her," I amend, my fierce stare begging him to argue.

"Glad you put the bottle down, man. I was tired of dealing with your arrogant brother. At least with you, I know what the fuck you intend to do. With him…" He frowns. "With him, I don't know what to think."

I'm not about to buddy up to Phoenix Nikolaides of all people and share a drink gossiping like two teenage girls over how much my brother is a sneaky bastard. No, I can think about that all by myself.

"Where's my money?" I demand, putting an end to all things Talia related.

He rolls his eyes like the fucking teenager I pegged him for and pulls out his phone. "I'll wire it over right now."

"I know, Selene," Aris grits out, his voice booming from his office. "I said I know, dammit."

Her annoying, screeching voice can be heard all the way into the hallway. I lean toward the door, hoping to catch her end of the conversation, but I hear nothing.

"Is that all?" he asks in a bored tone. "I have shit to do."

She must end the call because he slams the phone down on his desk and curses. I choose that moment to saunter in. He shoots me a weary look and then sighs heavily when I sit in front of his desk.

"Trouble in paradise?" I ask as I rest my ankle on my knee and lean back.

Ignoring me, he stands and checks the clock. "Your meeting with Phoenix went quickly. Back before five? Was he even there?"

"We had lunch and took care of business. He's not a cheating bastard like his weasel father."

Aris is rigid as he pours two drinks. When he sets down the tumbler with amber liquid in it, I pick up my glass and inhale the familiar scent.

"What's the special occasion?" I ask, swirling the alcohol around in the glass, eyeing him.

"Can't a man enjoy a nice bourbon with his brother and not need an excuse?" He knocks back the drink and dips his head, indicating for me to do the same.

I set it down and push it across the desk to him. "You look like you need it more than me."

His jaw clenches and he picks up the glass, slamming it back as well. "What do you want, Kostas?"

"My wife."

He tenses. "What the fuck do you want me to do about it?"

I shrug. "You asked me what I wanted. I told you. No need to get defensive."

"I'm not defensive," he growls.

I grew up with you, motherfucker. Don't play games with me. I taught them to you.

"Hmm," is all I say. "How come you never invite me over for these wonderful dinners your blow-up doll wannabe wife is always making?"

"I've invited you more times than I can count over the past year," he bites out. "Not my fault you chose to drink your dinner instead."

"Yes."

"Yes, what?"

"I accept your dinner invitation."

His gaze hardens. "You called my future fiancée a blow-up doll. Consider the invitation officially rescinded."

I lean forward in my seat. "Are you hiding something from me, brother?"

"Fuck off," he scoffs. "If you want to come to dinner, come to fucking dinner. Don't say I didn't warn you that Selene is a terrible goddamn cook and you'll probably die of food poisoning. Just make sure you give me a proper warning so she can get to the store and buy what she needs."

I stare at him for a long moment, watching him intently. Each facial tick. Every twitch of his lips. The slow reddening of his skin. Finally, once I've infuriated him to the point his carotid bounces along his neck, I stand.

"I'll let you know." I give him a wide grin that I know unnerves him. "Tell Selene I said hello."

Walking out of his office, I wonder how exactly he and Selene have made it this long. What does she offer him that makes him stay? He doesn't like her. At best, he barely tolerates her. Sure, she has tits and dick sucking lips, but you can find nicer women with those same physical attributes who don't sound like a donkey in heat.

I'm going to find out.

I settle back in my own office. Back to scouring video surveillance footage from the time Talia was with me around the time she was taken.

Taken.

I know it deep in my gut.

She wouldn't leave me.

Talia Demetriou may have been pissed as fuck, but she

loved me. She may have never spoken the words, but I felt them. Now that my head is clearing, I remember that part of our relationship without a doubt. With each look, each caress, each kiss, I knew.

And whoever took her will pay so fucking dearly for every second I've lost with her.

"I'm out of here," Aris says, peeking his head into my office. "Sorry about earlier. Selene is a bitch and she pisses me off."

"She must give amazing head," I say with a wicked smile.

He sneers. "I wish."

With a wave, he bolts before I can taunt him anymore.

So, the blow-up doll doesn't even suck cock well. Again, I wonder what the fuck sort of value she provides my brother with. He can get any fucking woman into his bed with his stupid smiles and charm. He certainly doesn't hang onto any woman for very long, much less a bitch like Selene. It's more than sex with my brother. It always is. I've seen him fuck the wife of a local gangster just to piss him off. I've seen him fuck around with the Minister of Police's daughter just to anger our father. I've seen him flirt with my wife and grab her ass because he wants to irritate me.

But Selene?

What's the end game?

Marriage, babies, white picket fence.

Yeah, fucking right.

I don't buy it for a second.

Swiveling around in my chair, I decide to dig into Selene a little. I'll find out what the blow-up doll has been up to. If the past year has taught me anything, it's that I can be quite the resourceful stalker when I want to be. I will tear apart Selene's past and present. I'll learn every damn detail about her. Who her family is. Who she's connected to. How she remains tethered to my brother.

And then I'll invite myself to fucking dinner.

chapter
six

Talia

TODAY IS THE DAY. I'VE SPENT THE LAST YEAR learning everything I can about where I am and what it will take to get out. I can either keep waiting, or I can make my move. At this point, I don't think there's any more preparing I can do. If it weren't for my precious cargo, I would've already tried to run, but with her in tow, I have to be twice as careful. I can't risk anything happening to her.

I'm sitting on the lounge chair out by the pool like I always am. Zoe is sleeping on the chair next to me on her belly, under the umbrella, sucking on her pacifier. My little girl loves the pool and sun. I bet she'll love the beach as well.

"I'm leaving for work," Aris says. "Do you need anything while I'm out?"

"I can have Selene pick up anything I need." I wave him off, knowing full well he won't let that happen anymore.

"She's not running any more errands for you," he says, just like I knew he would. "I'd hate for you and Selene to get into it again, and I come home to a bloodbath, so whatever you need, I'll pick it up."

Exactly what I was hoping he would say.

"Zoe hasn't been feeling well. Can you stop by the pharmacy to pick her up Tylenol?"

Aris's gaze lands on Zoe.

"She's teething," I add.

Her body shifts, and her pacifier falls from her lips, landing on the ground. I lean over to grab it, but I can't reach. "Can you hand me that, please?"

Aris picks it up off the floor and offers it back to me.

"It's dirty now." I shake my head. "Just throw it in the sink on your way out. I need to clean it before I give it back to her."

He shoves it into his front pocket. "What the hell does teething mean?"

I roll my eyes at his lack of parental knowledge. "It means she has teeth coming in and it hurts. Tylenol will help the pain."

"Fine, whatever. I'll pick it up on my way home."

"What time will that be?" When he glares, I add, "There are a lot of different kinds. I need you to take a picture of the different ones and send them to Selene so I can let you know which one."

Aris groans. "All right, I'll send her the pictures when I'm there. It probably won't be until five or six o'clock. I have a late meeting."

Perfect!

"Thank you," I say, dismissing him.

I wait for him to acknowledge his daughter before he walks away, but as always he doesn't. He never hugs or kisses or gives her any attention. Not that I'm complaining. I'd rather him stay the hell away from both of us. It's just that I find it odd. I think back to when I told him I was pregnant. In life, we have choices to make, and a lot of times when making a choice, it isn't about which choice is the right one, but which one will keep you alive…

"What the hell is wrong with you?" Selene screeches.

I lift my head from the inside of the toilet and glare at her. "Get out," I demand.

When she doesn't leave, I reach over and slam the door in her face, so I can finish throwing up in peace.

A few minutes later, I hear yelling in the other room. Aris must be home and he and Selene must be arguing. They're always arguing. Tiptoeing out to eavesdrop, I listen to what they're saying.

"You never said you planned to keep her here forever!" Selene whisper-yells. She's meaning to whisper, but her screeching voice carries.

"It's not forever," Aris explains. "It's only until my brother completely loses his shit and I take over the business. It's only been a month and my brother is already on a downward spiral."

"Then what are you going to do with her?"

"I haven't decided yet."

"Why don't you just kill her?" Selene whines. When Aris doesn't say anything, she says, "Aris…you don't like, like her, do you?"

"No, I don't like her, but I'm not going to kill her. Then I would be as much of a monster as my brother and father. Plus, she's pregnant, and it's either my baby or my brother's."

Oh my God! He knows! He knows I'm pregnant.

"She's what?" Selene screeches.

"Are you that fucking stupid?" Aris accuses. "Haven't you seen her throwing up since we brought her here?"

"And it could be yours?" Selene sounds like she's crying.

"Yes, now stop asking fucking questions. I need to go check

on her. When I come back, you need to be waiting for me in bed, with your legs spread and your mouth closed."

Footsteps across the wood floor have me scrambling back to my room. I've just dropped onto my bed, when Aris enters the room.

"Did you hear all of that?" he asks. My eyes widen in shock. "Good, then I don't have to repeat myself. You're pregnant. You know it and I know it. The question is, who is the father?"

I have a choice to make…right here, right now. If I tell him the baby is his, he can take it from me after he or she's born. If I say it's Kostas's, his hatred toward his brother can lead to him hurting it. Either way, I'm possibly screwed…

"It's yours," I admit.

"I call bullshit."

"Call it whatever you want." I shrug.

"If I find out you're lying, you will pay," he threatens.

"More than what I am now?" I challenge. "How long do you plan to keep this up, Aris? You know I heard you…you're not going to kill me, so what are you going to do? Keep me prisoner forever?" I scoff. "It's not like Kostas loves me. It was an arranged marriage." But even as I say the words, I refuse to believe them myself.

Aris chuckles darkly. "If you believe that, you're either dumb or blind. Until you, I didn't think my dear brother was even capable of loving anyone besides our mother, but I was wrong, which is why I took you."

"You took me because you think he loves me?" I don't get it. There has to be more to it.

"I took you because my brother destroys everything he touches and he's not going to get a chance to destroy you the way he destroyed our mother."

"Aris…" I begin, but I don't even know what to say. I hate

him. He raped me. He hurt me. He stole me. But my heart still breaks for the man who lost his mother. He's grieving and he's broken. He's not thinking clearly. My only hope is that he'll eventually come to his senses and let me go. And hopefully before this baby is born.

That was a year ago. He was a monster the day he took me, but now, it's as if he lives for destroying Kostas. He feeds off it. He's never going to let me go, which means I have no option but to run.

Zoe's tiny body stretches, telling me she's waking up. Her fisted hands rise above her head, and her chunky little body rolls to the side. Her beautiful blue eyes open and she grants me the most beautiful smile.

"Mommy's going to get us out of here, *cara mia*."

After I feed her and give her a bath, I get dressed in a comfortable outfit. I don't have any tennis shoes, so I make do with the pair of flip flops I have. I tie my hair back in a ponytail and then pull my bag out from under my bed.

When I tiptoe out of the room, I spot Selene on the couch watching TV. I need to be smart about this. Aris's dumb ass gave her a fucking gun. If I play this right, that gun can become an asset to me, but if it goes the other way, it can be the very thing that kills me.

I spot the gun on the end table next to her. Laying my bag down behind the counter, near the garage door, I set Zoe in her high chair. "Be a good girl," I whisper, placing a few cereal puffs on her tray.

"Hey, Selene," I call out.

"What?"

"Aris is supposed to text you a picture of the different Tylenols for Zoe when he's on his way home. Has he texted you yet?"

"No." Good, that means he's still at work. I have time.

Grabbing a frying pan from under the sink—yes, I'm about to be cliché as hell—I tiptoe up to Selene. I'm not sure if the pan will actually knock her out, but my intention is just to knock her off her game long enough to grab the gun. Once I have it, I can make a run for it and she won't be able to stop me.

I spot her phone in her lap. I want to grab it as well, but the gun is more important. Raising the heavy item to the side, I swing it as hard as I can at the side of her head.

"Ahhh!" she screams, falling from the couch and onto the floor. Without looking back at her, I snatch the gun off the table, dart back to the dining room, grab my daughter and bag, and haul ass. I quickly type in the code to the garage and it works! Using the key in my hand, I hit the fob to unlock the doors. The SUV lights up and I throw Zoe into the seat next to me. I hate that I don't have a car seat for her, but there's nothing I can do. With a click of the garage door, it rises, and we're free.

chapter
seven

Kostas

"**B**ASIL?"

Adrian nods at my question as he pulls into the driveway of my father's estate. Once we're in park, he levels me with a hard glare. "Basil is loyal until the end."

There was a time when I almost questioned Basil's loyalties. When he did my brother's bidding. But when I'd looked in his eyes, I'd seen he was simply doing his job. For me. At the time, it felt like betrayal, but he was only doing what I'd asked long before.

Keep the enemies close.

And since I've always seen Aris as an enemy who happens to share my blood, my two best men, Basil and Adrian, have always kept an extra close eye on him.

"Any news from Basil then?" I ask, climbing out of Adrian's SUV.

He follows me and lets out a grunt. "Just normal comings and goings to and from the hotel. His house is pretty quiet during the day. On occasion, his slut leaves to grocery shop and shit."

"Galani? Niles? Does anyone besides the skank go in and out?"

"Nope, just her."

I don't like it. Feels too easy.

"Call him and have him see if he can find anything out from the hotel staff. I want this quiet and discreet. He'll need to do it in person."

"I'll text him and send him that way," Adrian assures me. "You sure dropping in on your dad like this is okay? What if we're interrupting his nap?"

I bite back a snort of laughter. Adrian, even though he's one of my best men, has always been more like a brother to me than Aris ever was. He's the only motherfucker I'll allow to get away with making fun of my father.

"Good to keep the old man on his toes," I say with a chuckle.

We walk through the massive estate looking for him. Things are strained with my father. He thinks I should run things differently than I do, but I do them the way I want and there's nothing he can do about it. He is my father, though, so I don't disrespect him by just ignoring him. I make sure he's taken care of and check in on him from time to time like a good son does.

When I hear moans coming from down the hallway, I pause to shoot Adrian a confused look. I stalk down the hall to the source of the sound. At my father's door, I hesitate for a fraction of a second before pushing into the room. The sight before me has bile crawling up my throat.

Some young blond bitch is riding my father in my parents' bed. He may not be able to walk, but his big hands dig into her pale ass as he urges her to fuck him. She moans and rocks her hips. All I can do is see fucking red. My mother has barely been dead a year and he's fucking sluts in their bed.

"Father," I boom. "What the fuck?"

The woman cries out in surprise and slides off him. Her big tits bounce as she scrambles to find her dress that's been discarded on the floor. I stand there glaring at my father, who looks like a pathetic old man with his dick at half-mast.

"The money's in the usual place, Lyssa," he grumbles out, his eyes cutting to mine as he pulls the covers over himself. "Why the hell are you here unannounced?"

Money?

My father is fucking a goddamn prostitute?

I block the doorway when the blonde comes my way. She casts a glance over at Father, as if to ask him what she's supposed to do.

"A whore, Father? Really?" I guess it's better than him actually dating so soon after my mother. The fact it's just sex seems to soften the blow a little. Still pisses me off. Feels like just yesterday my mother was buried.

"Lyssa is more than a whore," Father bites out. "She's a friend. We go way back."

Pull the fucking brakes. "What?"

"What'd I miss?" Aris demands from behind me, finally gracing us with his presence. "Fucking gross. Do I smell pussy in Dad's room?"

Father's face burns red with fury when Aris scoots past me and into the room. My brother shakes his head.

"Why are you two here?" Father barks out.

"Kostas said we should meet with you," Aris says, his gaze raking down Lyssa. "Who are you?"

"Father's whore," I hiss.

"Another one?" Aris asks.

I snap my head his way. "What do you mean another one?"

Aris sneers at me. "Why are you acting like this is the first one you knew about?"

Darting my eyes back to my father, I fist my hands. "So Mamá dies and you fuck as many whores as you can? I didn't think your dick even worked anymore."

Aris snorts. "Since Mamá died? Where the hell have you been all our lives, man?"

All our lives?

He's fucking with me.

Our mother may have cheated on Father, but my father was loyal to her. He's the whole goddamn reason why I'm so obsessed with loyalty. It's been drilled into my head for as long as I can remember.

"Lyssa's been on the payroll for years, Kostas. Don't be obtuse." My father scowls my way.

Obtuse?

Don't be fucking obtuse?

The woman in question shrugs as if it's no big deal to fuck a man three times her age who can't even go to the bathroom by himself.

"What about Mamá?" I hiss.

Father's face softens. "I know you're having a rough time since your wife left you—"

"She didn't fucking leave me," I roar, making the woman jump.

Aris seems pleased as hell to see me lose my shit over our father's indiscretions. The smile is wiped off his face when his phone rings. As he scrambles to pull his phone from his pocket, something hits the floor and bounces. A pacifier. For a baby. I stare at it in confusion as he picks it up and shoves it back in his pocket. He answers the phone in a hateful tone that makes me wonder, again, if he even likes that woman he's shacked up with. His dumbass bitch can be heard screeching on the other line. He pales and then pure fury morphs the charming Demetriou prince into a dragon. For a split second, his hateful eyes find mine, and if they had the power, he'd slay me where I stand.

"Emergency with Selene," he growls out as he pushes past me, knocking his shoulder into mine on the way out.

Lyssa takes his exit as her cue to leave as well. As she steps past me, I grab her bicep. She shoots me a panicked look.

"You fucked him while he was married to my mother?" I demand in a cold tone.

Her eyes flicker over to my father, but he doesn't save or defend her. I can see it in her eyes. The answer is clear as day. Yes.

"Lyssa is a tigress in bed, son. You can't tell me you haven't fucked anyone since Talia left."

"She. Didn't. Leave. Talia was taken."

"And with all those pretty maids walking around, you're telling me you didn't get your dick sucked not once this entire time?"

"I'm fucking married, Father!"

He snorts. "Marriage is something for everyone else to see. It's an illusion of happiness. Everyone fucks around. Even me."

But what about loyalty to your motherfucking wife? He's drilled loyalty into my head since I was old enough to learn what the word meant. It was all a fucking lie.

"Adrian," I bark out.

His heavy footsteps thud down the hall. "Sir?"

"Take Lyssa home. The *long* way."

He doesn't argue or balk at my orders. Adrian's a good man. Without explanation, he'll do what needs doing and that's burying this dirty little secret today.

I release her once he has her in his grip. He stalks away with her. My gaze falls to the stack of bills on the dresser—money she'll never touch again.

"You lied to me," I tell him, bitterness creeping into my tone. "My entire life I thought you were devoted to my mother."

"Don't be an idiot," he bites out. "You know your mother slept with Niles fucking Nikolaides of all people."

I couldn't understand it before. How she'd even step out of her marriage in the first place. But now I wonder. Did she know about my father's whores? Was she trying to hurt him like he hurt her?

"When did you take your first whore after marriage?" I ask, my voice deadly and cold.

He glowers at me and his jaw clenches. My eyes skirt over to the pillow beside him. My mother's pillow. A smear of Lyssa's lipstick taints the pillowcase. A framed picture of my mother on the nightstand faces the bed as though she's punished even in death to take my father's abuse.

"This is none of your business," he says, cutting through my thoughts.

Slamming my gaze back on his, I crack my neck. "Everything's my business now."

His nostrils flare at my words. The double meaning behind them. "I'm still in charge here," he seethes. "You're my son, but you mustn't forget who built this empire from the ground up."

His skin is grayish and his muscle tone is gone. Father is

nothing but a decaying bag of bones. It's a wonder his dick still works because his legs sure as fuck don't. He's a pathetic excuse for a man lying in his bed, unable to do a goddamn thing but listen to what I have to say.

"You're not in charge," I state coolly. "I've been running this shit ever since the accident last year."

"Accident? Your mother's attempted murder was an accident?"

"You provoked her," I bark.

"You're insane, boy."

I crack my neck again before sliding my jacket off and draping it over the back of his wheelchair. His eyes track my movements. When I unbutton my shirt at the cuff, he narrows his gaze.

"You're going to beat an old man up? What kind of son are you?" Despite his rage, fear glimmers in his eyes.

I slowly roll my sleeve up to my elbow. The muscles in my forearm flex and the veins throb with the need to inflict pain.

"You're my father," I hiss. "I'd never strike you."

He relaxes some, but his weary gaze remains fixed on my actions. I take my time rolling up my other sleeve as well.

"This is my empire, Kostas. *I* am the Demetriou name. You can't forget that," he tells me with false bravado.

"What happens when you're gone?" I ask, already knowing the answer. "That's right, everything goes to me."

"To both my sons," he lies.

Now that I don't have the alcohol buzzing through me and wreaking havoc on my brain, I took the time this morning to analyze every facet of my life. According to our family attorney, I'm still listed as sole heir to the hotels, the Demetriou fortune, everyfuckingthing.

"I used to think loyalty was the backbone of our family name." I make a tsk of disapproval. "I was wrong. It's lies. Lies are woven into every aspect of our lives like fucking snakes in a garden." I smile at him. "It's time to cut the head off the biggest viper in the nest."

"You won't cut me open like I'm one of our victims in the cellar," he growls. "I know you better than that, Kostas. In case you've forgotten, I'm your father. We're exactly the same."

"You're right," I admit. "I won't make you bleed." My gaze drifts to my mother's picture. "But where you're wrong is that we're not the same. You may have destroyed Mamá, but you will not destroy me." I flash the picture a sinister smile. "This is for what you couldn't finish, Mamá. I heard your dying wishes loud and clear. I won't let you down."

"What the f—"

Father's words are silenced when I reach across him to grab Mamá's pillow that's stained with another woman's lipstick. I shove the fluffy pillow down on his face. His attempts to drag the pillow away and then trying to hit at me are futile. I'm a monster. A motherfucking fire-breathing beast. He's a lowly snake in the grass waiting to be stomped on. With my eyes on my mother's picture, I smother my father with her pillow. He should have died when she shot him. It's my duty to end the disloyal bastard's existence. My father struggles for longer than I expect given his weakened state. I'll give him that. At one time, I thought he was the most powerful man in the world. I fucking looked up to him. And the way he looked after Mamá and loved her was admirable.

Lies.

All lies.

Mamá may have broken my heart when she killed

54

herself, but she opened my eyes. She tugged on the veil of deception my father had slipped over my head. She made me see there was more to life than money and mayhem.

Love.

She wanted me to see that love was more important than so called loyalty.

It was hard to believe considering she'd deceived my father, but now learning he was the root of everything, I feel as though I finally understand her message.

Love is everything.

Love is loyalty and forgiveness and hope.

The rest is just bullshit.

I'm not sure how long I hold the pillow over Father's face, but when he's stopped moving for some time, I pull the pillow away and gently put it back where it goes beside him. His eyes are glazed over but still open. I slide my fingers down over his lids, closing them. When I check his pulse, I learn he's, in fact, dead.

I feel nothing.

Not victory or sadness.

Fucking nothing.

Once I undo my sleeves, I pull my jacket back on. I grab the picture of my mother and then head downstairs. As I wait for Adrian to return to pick me up, I make some coffee and sit in the kitchen on a barstool. My mind drifts to times when Mamá would busy herself in here, despite the fact we had a cook, and try to give us some semblance of a normal life. She'd sing and teasingly brush flour on my nose as we baked together whenever Father was away on business. I loved those simple moments with her. When I forgot I was destined to be a mob boss and could just be her little boy. Back when I would dream of racing cars in Monte

Carlo and surfing with sharks. I was innocent and my father ripped that innocence away from me no matter how hard my mother clutched me to her, trying to preserve it.

I'm not innocent anymore.

But it doesn't mean I can't be the man my mother would have wanted me to be.

I'll never be good, that's for damn sure. I'll be good enough for love, though, just as she would have wanted. I'm good enough for Talia. And one day soon I'll find her.

"Good afternoon," Tammy, a nurse of Father's, greets as she enters. "How's Ezio?"

I clench my jaw and think about my mother. About how devastated I was when she pulled that trigger on herself. Real emotion shines in my eyes as I regard the nurse.

"He went to be with Mamá during his nap," I choke out.

"Oh, honey," Tammy cries out. "He died?"

I nod and the woman hugs me. I let her. To be honest, it feels good to be drawn in a motherly hug. Resting my chin on top of her gray head, I let out a heavy sigh.

"You know Father. He's so proud. It was his wish to keep his death quiet when the time came. Cremation. No service."

She pulls away and furrows her brows as she cups my cheeks. "I'm discreet, honey. We'll get it sorted together. Just tell me what I need to do."

"Let me be the one to tell my brother," I mutter. "To tell everyone."

"Do what you have to do, dear. I'll go upstairs and make sure he's decent."

"Thanks, Tammy. Don't worry about not getting paid. I'll have Aris wire you a bonus as a thank you for all you've done."

She smiles at me. "The Demetriou men are good men. I'm proud to have worked for this family."

We're bad men, but I don't want to spoil the moment with the truth.

I give her a nod, dismissing her. I sip on my coffee as I watch out the window for Adrian. It takes a quick call to Franco to have him come deal with Father's body, and another call to the family attorney, Thomas, to inform him of the official change of power. The next person to know needs to be Aris. And it'll need to be told in person. No one wants to hear their father is dead over the phone.

I'll go back to the office, deal with some other affairs, and then drop by this evening to deliver the news over dinner. Kill two birds with one stone. It's time to see what lies Aris has been telling, and if I know my brother, the lies are plentiful. I've just never really cared too much until now.

But now?

Now I care a whole lot.

I'm going to uncover every hidden truth.

And once everything is all laid out on the table, I'm going to make those who've been playing games against me pay.

Blood. Sweat. Tears. Limbs.

They. Will. Pay.

Every last one of them.

chapter
eight

Talia

As I drive down the driveway, the winding road takes us to the front gate. I hold my breath, praying it opens from the inside. Over the last year, I've planned the best I could, but because I couldn't see this far, I could only plan to leave. As the gate slowly moves to the side, I spot a black SUV driving up behind me. What the hell? There's no way Selene caught up that fast. When I glance in my rearview mirror, I spot a man in the driver's seat.

Without waiting for the gate to completely open, I press my foot on the gas, refusing to let this guy, whoever he is, catch up to us. Damn it! How did I not see him? Aris must have someone guarding the house, but he's never been where I can see him. I've checked so many times.

Zoe sits in the passenger seat, babbling to me, as I drive down the curvy roads. I have no clue where I am or where I'm going, but my goal is to get to the city so I can ask someone for help.

I look in the mirror again, and the SUV is catching up

to me. There's no way I'm going to make it out of these hills unless I pick up my speed. I glance over at my little girl and she smiles up at me. I need to protect her. I need to get us to safety.

With one hand on the wheel, I reach over and grab the seatbelt, drawing it across her lap. It's not ideal, but it's the best I can do in a shitty situation. I press my foot harder on the gas and increase my speed, but when I glance back, the SUV is less than a car away from me now. I'm never going to make it.

All this work, all this planning, and I missed something. I slam my fist against the steering wheel. I was so fucking close. Aris is never going to give me this much leeway again. I had one chance and I messed it up.

The front of the SUV hits my back bumper and the vehicle swerves.

No!

My eyes briefly fly to Zoe to make sure she's okay before they're back on the road.

I can do this. I can get away.

He lays down on the horn. He wants me to pull over. I make it around the bend before his bumper hits mine again. Zoe lurches forward and I use my hand to hold her against the seat. I can't keep going. Whoever this guy is isn't going to stop until I pull over, and I can't risk him driving me off the road. I can't put my daughter's life in jeopardy.

Prickly tears of defeat burn in my eyes as my heart rate races.

I don't want to give up. I'm not ready to give up.

When my gaze flits back over to my little girl, my eyes land on the gun in the center console, and my thoughts go to Kostas. He wouldn't even hesitate. If he were in my shoes right now, he would kill this asshole. It's me and Zoe or him. And I'm choosing me and Zoe.

I can do this.

I am Talia Demetriou, wife of a fucking mob boss.

I pull over on the side of the road and get out, not wanting him to make it over to where my daughter is. I flip the safety off and wait for him to exit the vehicle. And when he does, I'm momentarily stunned. Estevan Galani. The man my husband shot in the dick. Of course Aris would hire a damn enemy to guard his house. Those two roaches deserve each other. At least one of them is about to be exterminated. Kostas can deal with Aris.

Pointing the gun right at him, I pull the trigger.

Pop!

The gunshot echoes loudly, making my ears ring and Zoe scream. He stumbles back, but doesn't fall. Fucking damn roach. Crimson swells where I clipped his shoulder.

"You bitch!" he growls, pulling his own gun out.

Before he has a chance to hurt either one of us, I pull the trigger again and again and again. Until he hits the ground. I stare in shock at the bullet holes littering his chest.

I shot him.

I fucking shot him.

My hands are shaking, and my body is numb. I just killed a man. One who would've done the same to me, I remind myself. As I turn around to run back to my vehicle, I run right into a hard wall. No, not a wall…

"That wasn't very smart," Aris says.

I lift the gun to shoot him, but before I can, he snatches it out of my hand.

"Get your daughter from the vehicle, now," he barks, "and get your ass in my car."

My eyes dart around me, wondering if there's any way I can still escape. There are woods on both sides, but there's no way I'll make it to grab Zoe and run without Aris stopping me.

As if reading my thoughts, he snarls, "Don't even think about it. Get your fucking ass in the car."

We walk a few feet, when I hear a moaning sound. That asshole is seriously not dead?

Aris hits me with a hard glare, then stalks over to him. With the same gun I used, he points it at Estevan's forehead and shoots. His brains explode, and I lose everything in my stomach.

Everything's a blur as I pull Zoe from the seat and clutch her to my chest. I can feel the tears falling, but I'm numb to them. I sit in the front seat of Aris's Porsche and inhale my sweet baby's hair.

Please don't hurt us.

Please don't hurt us.

Zoe is no longer crying now that I'm soothing her, and she babbles to Aris when he falls into the front seat. He says something to her before peeling out and taking us back in the direction we came. When we get back to the house, Selene is sitting on the couch with an icepack pressed to the side of her head.

"You fucking bitch!" she hisses.

"Enough!" Aris booms. "I have to go clean up the fucking mess you made," he says to me. "And since you can't play nice with Selene, and I can't risk you trying to escape, you can now consider yourself a prisoner."

"Oh, *now* I can?" I scoff. "I've been your damn prisoner for the last year."

Aris smirks wickedly. "No, Talia, you were my guest. Now, you're about to see what it means to be my prisoner." He forces me into my room and I set Zoe in her crib, so I can deal with him, but when I turn around, the door is slammed shut and it's locked from the outside. Motherfucker! I race through the bathroom to see if that door is unlocked, but as I twist the knob, the lock clicks in place. He locked me inside! With a hopeless sigh, I slide down the door and press my head against the wood. This was it. This was my one chance. And it's gone. And now we're worse off than before.

Zoe's babbling has me standing and going to her. Lifting her out of her crib, I bring her over to my bed and lay her next to me. Holding her tight, I stroke her soft black hair until her eyes flutter closed and she falls asleep, and then I let myself fall asleep as well.

Knock. Knock. Knock.

My eyes shoot back open.

Knock. Knock. Knock.

Is someone knocking on the door? Nobody ever knocks on the door. Carefully edging off the bed, so I don't wake Zoe, I go to the window to see who's there. I can't see the front door, but I can see part of the driveway.

Maserati GranTurismo.

Charcoal-gray.

Black on black tires.

It can't be… There's only one man I know who has that exact car…

Kostas.

He's here. He's going to save us.

And just like that my hope is restored. Like a sliver of light illuminating my dark world, I can finally see again. I'm chasing it. Running toward the brightness.

I don't bother trying to open the window because I already know it's nailed shut, but I watch the vehicle, refusing to look anywhere else. The house is quiet. Selene must be outside talking to him. Does he know I'm here? I listen with bated breath until I hear the front door close.

Is he in here? I can't decide whether to abandon the window to go bang on the door, or stay by the window to catch a glimpse of him. Before I make a decision, though, I see him. In his signature suit, he stalks back to his car. Strong, powerful, handsome. I miss him so much it hurts. My palms hit the glass, hoping he will somehow hear me.

"Kostas!" I cry out, knowing it's futile.

His hand freezes on the handle, and he turns. Did he hear me?

"Kostas!" I yell again, my palms smacking so hard against the window, they're stinging. "Kostas! I'm here!"

His eyes assess the area before he opens the door and folds himself into his car. And then he's gone. And as quickly as the light came, it's now gone. Leaving me stumbling through the darkness alone.

A flood of tears gush down my cheeks as I watch my fucking husband's headlights get farther and farther away until they're completely gone.

One year and he's never been here. And when he finally does show up, I'm locked in my fucking room. He must know something. That's why he came here. He's looking for me. I know he is.

Oh, Kostas, you're so close. Don't give up, please. I'm here, waiting for you.

Crawling back to my bed, I snuggle back up with Zoe. She's awake now from me yelling, but as soon as I comfort her, she falls back asleep. Such a good girl. She deserves more than this. More than being held prisoner.

"It's okay, *cara mia*, we're going to be saved."

"Wake up," Aris barks. His voice startles Zoe and she lets out a loud cry. I glare daggers his way, but he doesn't care. "It's time to eat."

"I'm not hungry. I'll eat later."

"You'll eat now, or you won't eat at all," he threatens.

After changing Zoe's diaper, I grab a bottle to bring out to the table. When I get out there, Selene and Aris are both at the table, already eating their dinner. Steak, broccoli, and potatoes au gratin. He must've brought it home because Selene can barely make grilled cheese without burning the shit out of it.

When I walk past the table, Aris's hand lands on my thigh. "I'm going to grab a jar of food for Zoe."

"I'll get it," he says. "Sit down."

"Fine." I set Zoe in her high chair and place a bib around her neck. She giggles her delight, slapping her tray in excitement.

Aris brings over a jar of sweet potatoes and a spoon and sets them in front of Zoe before sitting back down. Zoe grabs the spoon and bangs it against her tray. "Da-da-da," she babbles. Aris's eyes meet mine. "Da-da," she continues. She's too young to know what she's saying. She's just making random noises, but the thought that she's calling him da-da has me feeling sick to my stomach.

I open the jar and begin feeding it to Zoe, when Aris finally speaks. "Until further notice, you will be locked in your room while I'm not home."

"Are you seriously going to keep me and your *daughter* locked in a room for hours at a time?" I shoot him a glare.

"Or I can have Selene take care of her and just keep *you* locked up…" Aris smirks with a shrug.

Selene huffs, and when I look at her, the entire side of her face is black and blue. I can't help the grin that splays across my face. That pan got her good.

"Fuck you," she spits. "Hope it was worth it."

"Oh, it was," I volley. "Looks like you're going to be needing another visit to the plastic surgeon. Probably for the best since they fucked up your face the first time around anyway."

"Aris, haven't you had enough of this bitch? Your brother was here today! He's snooping around and he's going to find her."

My gaze swings over to Aris, whose eyes widen.

"Kostas was here?" he growls, venom in his tone. "Why the fuck didn't you tell me?"

"I just did!" Selene screeches. "And he was asking questions. How long until he figures out you have his precious Talia? Just kill her already. We can take your baby and run."

At her words, I snatch the steak knife off the table and dart around behind her, putting her into a headlock before she can even think about what to do. With the knife against her throat, I meet Aris's gaze. "You let this woman touch my fucking baby and I will slice her throat."

"Enough," Aris stands. "Put the damn knife down." He steps toward me and I press the blade against Selene's throat.

"Aris!" she cries.

"Talia, calm down." Aris's eyes dart over to Zoe. When he steps toward her, I have no choice but to let go of Selene.

"Don't you touch her." With the knife still in my hand, I lift my daughter out of her high chair.

"She's my daughter too," Aris sneers. "And if I want to fucking touch her, I will."

He steps toward me and I take a step back. When he doesn't make another move, I continue backing up until I'm back in my room.

"We'll deal with this tomorrow," Aris says. "Clearly shit needs to change around here."

Without saying another word to him, I slam the door in his face, and then I pray to God that Kostas comes back for me and Zoe. Because if he doesn't, I'm not sure how much longer Aris is going to keep me alive.

chapter
nine

Kostas

I'M SEEING SHIT.

    Losing my goddamn mind.

    It. Was. Her.

I pinch the bridge of my nose and debate on what to do next. Either I can drive my ass back over to Aris's house and find out for sure, or I can sit here like a pussy wondering.

I'm just downing the rest of my dinner in a restaurant between the hotel and Aris's, when my phone rings. I could answer it and tell him right now that Father is dead. Most days, I'm a dick, but even I won't do that to him. No, I'll do like I intended when I drove over there earlier and tell him to his face. I send his call to voicemail. Seconds later, I get a text.

Aris: Did you come by?

The next text comes immediately after.

Aris: What did you need?

Aris: Want to meet up?

I groan and before I can reply, he continues blowing up my phone.

Aris: Selene said you had something important to talk about.

Aris: I don't hit her if that's what you're wondering. She fell.

Fell?

I'm not stupid. That bitch did more than fall. Someone bashed her fucking head in.

My mind drifts to earlier.

"What do you want?"

I lift my brow and sneer. "Excuse me?"

"How did you even get on the property?"

"I used the fucking code," I growl. "Were you trying to keep me out?"

Selene has the sense to stand down once she remembers who she's talking to and shakes her head in vehemence. I'm not some pushover like Aris. I will drag her skinny ass back to the cellar by her fake-red hair to remind her if I need to. Luckily, she replaces her snotty expression with one of healthy fear.

"What'd you do to your face?" I ask, nodding to indicate the giant ass bruise that looks fresh and is forming beneath her swollen-red flesh.

She purses her fat lips before letting out a huff of exasper-ation. "I fell."

Says every woman hiding the fact she's being hit by a man.

"The floor must fucking hate you."

"And I hate the fucking floor too," she snarls out. "Aris went to…run an errand. Is there something I can help you

with?" Her venom bleeds away as her green eyes skim down the front of my body in appreciation.

"Nah," I grunt out. "I'll come by another time."

When I turn to leave, she grips my bicep. "Call him first."

I glower over my shoulder at her. "Are you his keeper?"

"W-What? No. He's just always busy and rarely home. You should call him first so you don't miss him."

"Hmmm," is all I say before breaking from her hold and walking away.

The door slams shut behind me. I'm almost to my car when I feel eyes on me. Stopping, I turn and look back toward Aris's massive house.

Blond hair.

A woman.

Talia?

But when I squint, the vision vanishes. That's all she is to me now. A fucking ghost.

God, I miss her. I'd give up my entire fortune to have her in my arms just so I could inhale her hair. I don't know that I even remember what she smells like anymore. The fact I'd give up everything to see her once more is disappointing. I'd always thought of myself as someone powerful. Someone who doesn't need anyone else.

Like my father.

Turns out, I was never like him.

I was always like my mother.

After I pay my bill, I leave the restaurant and inhale the early fall air. The sun has gone down. It's only just hitting me that my father really is gone. I extinguished him from this earth. Remorse or guilt should flood through me, but all I feel is relief. I was never allowed to figure out who the real Kostas was. He bred me into his monster. For his favor over my brother, I gladly heeded every instruction. And now I'm nothing but a shell. I don't want to do anything but fill up my entire being with her.

My wife.

Fuck, I'm losing it.

I need to tell Aris Father is dead and then move the fuck on. At some point, I will have to accept that Talia probably is too. A year is a long time—too long in my world—to be missing without a word. If she'd run away, I would've known about it. Someone would have tattled.

She's dead.

It's a hard pill to swallow.

One I have trouble choking down because too much uncertainty rattles around inside my head.

I pull up to the gate and punch in the same four digits Aris uses for everything. It'd been a no-brainer when I'd come earlier, but after the way Selene acted, it made me wonder if they were trying to keep me away.

So I wouldn't see that he beats on her?

Like I give a shit. She probably runs her fucking mouth too much and earned that knock to the head. We're villains, not goddamn heroes. Who am I to judge?

No, if they wanted to keep me away, it's for other reasons.

Reasons that niggle and tug at me, desperate to be thrown out in the open.

I pull up to the house and park in the driveway. Lights shine from a window in front of the house and then some upstairs. Climbing out, I pause to listen. Nothing but the breeze picking up as a fall storm rolls in. The wind whistles and I scent the promise of rain.

As I walk toward the front door, my eyes drift of their own accord to the window where I'd thought I'd seen someone. When a figure stands in front of the glass, the light shining around them, my heart does a squeeze in my chest.

I blink several times to clear my vision.

Still there.

Blond hair. A woman.

I'm storming over to the window before I can stop myself. Wide, teary blue eyes meet mine. Familiar blue eyes. Her blue eyes.

No. Fucking. Way.

"*Zoí mou.*" My life.

Her bottom lip trembles—lips I've ached to kiss for so long it's maddening. This can't be real. She can't be staring back at me from behind the glass of Aris's fucking house. It makes no sense. I'm truly losing my goddamn mind.

"Kostas."

The voice of an angel carries through the glass, shattering what little bit was left of my heart. She's alive. She's alive and well and standing right in fucking front of me.

"Open the window," I rumble, my words barely a whisper.

She looks over her shoulder and shakes her head. "I can't."

Fury swells up inside me to incredible heights. "Open the fucking window."

Tears race down her cheeks as she moves her plump lips rapidly, speaking in hushed tones that are somehow supposed to send me away.

I'm not going anywhere.

Bending, I try to open the window, but it's locked shut.

I point at the lever and thump the glass hard. "Talia, unlock the window."

"I can't."

I slam my fist on the window, making her cry out in surprise.

"I said open the window or so help me I'm coming right through it," I growl. "Open it. Talia, open it!"

When she steps away, turning to look toward the door again, I lose it. With a swift swing of my elbow, I bust out a pane of glass. I reach my hand inside and flip the lock. It still won't open.

Talia rushes back over to me and reaches her hand through the glass pane. Her touch is soft as she runs her fingertips along my cheek. "I can't, Kostas. It's nailed shut."

Nailed shut.

What in the actual fuck?

I grip her wrist in a tight grip and then lean in to kiss her palm. I'm afraid to let her go because she might just fucking vanish again, but I need to get to her. I need to hold her.

"Stand back," I order.

She jerks her hand back and steps away from the window. I could go beat on the front door, make my brother answer, and demand he hand her over, but right now I'm on a one-track mission. Get to my fucking wife. Hiking my leg up, I kick hard along the metal strip along the middle of the window.

Crunch. Crunch. Crunch.

I kick over and over until the metal frame of the window is mutilated and folded in, glass broken all over at my feet. Once I've weakened it enough, I slam my shoulder into what's left of the window and send it and myself careening to the floor. I'm on my feet in the next second, prowling after Talia.

Anger. Betrayal. Sadness. Confusion.

My emotions spin around and around like a fucking tornado. I'm ready to cause massive destruction. I want to destroy everyone.

Gripping Talia's throat, I walk her back until her ass hits the door. I bury my nose in her hair, inhaling the scent of her shampoo mixed with her natural sweat. The growl rumbling through me is a possessive one bordering on rage. My thumb traces along the vein in her throat that's pulsing rapidly.

"Why?" It's the only word I have. It's a loaded question.

"I don't know."

I pull away and glower at her. "You want to be here?"

She shakes her head, fat tears rolling down her red cheeks.

"You're trapped here?"

A sob escapes her. "We have to get out of here."

I'm distracted by her bottom wobbly lip, and now that I know she's a captive for some fucked-up reason, I need her like I need my next breath.

"*Zoí mou*," I whisper over her lips. "I've fucking missed you."

Slamming my lips to hers, I take the kiss I've been craving since the moment I let her walk away from me after our fight. I slide my hand up to her jaw, gripping her tight so she can't escape me as I ravish her perfect mouth. She moans as I devour her lips and tongue. Her fingers thread through my hair, cradling me to her. My other hand finds her hip and I slide it to her ass that's fleshier than I remember. I want to strip her down right here and inspect every part of her body to see if she's changed. A choked sound escapes her when I rotate my hips, rubbing my aching cock against her body.

"Da-da-da-da."

I freeze mid-kiss. When I hear an excited shriek, I yank away from Talia, my head darting around to find the source. My eyes land on a baby. A fucking baby. With bright blue eyes like Talia.

Talia steps toward me. "Kostas, listen—"

"A baby?" I growl, snapping my head back to look at her.

Her chin is tilted up and her watery eyes are fierce. "My baby."

I stumble back, feeling as though she's kicked me in the gut. A baby. Her baby. And Aris's? The baby makes another sound and I can't help but look over at her.

"Kostas," she says, walking over to the baby and picking it up. "Her name is Zoe."

All the air is sucked from my lungs as I snap my eyes back to the little girl.

Zoe.

Zoe.

Zoe.

"Zoe, *zoí mou*?"

Tears well in her eyes and she nods rapidly.

Holy shit.

Our baby.

We had a fucking baby.

All happy thoughts come to a screeching halt. I'm going to murder them. Slaughter both Aris and Selene. Right the fuck now.

"Kostas," Talia says, her voice shaking as she rushes over to me. "We have to go. Now."

The baby—Zoe—grabs the lapel of my suit and tries to pull it her way. I'm stunned for so many fucking reasons. All I can do is lean forward and inhale her dark hair.

Mine.

She's fucking mine.

They both are.

I'm eerily calm as I say, "I'm going to kill them."

"And I want you to," she whispers. "But we need to get Zoe someplace safe. Selene has a gun and she's not afraid to use it."

My mind wars with what I should do. The mobster inside me craves violence and blood and vengeance. The husband—*and father*—in me has an overwhelming urge to protect what's mine.

I can't have both.

Not in this moment.

So I choose them.

Pressing a soft kiss to Talia's lips, I murmur, "Let's go."

She hands me Zoe and I freeze. I've never held a damn baby. But Talia doesn't give me a chance to argue. The moment the tiny flailing thing is in my arms, Talia starts throwing stuff into a diaper bag. I can't help but hold Zoe close to me, kissing the top of her head.

Those motherfuckers kept this from me.

My wife. My baby. My goddamn family.

Rage surges violently inside of me, but I don't unleash it. Talia's right. I need to get them out of here and make a plan. I'll get the full story of what's happened and then shed blood when my family is safe. Within minutes, Talia is packed and we head out the broken window. She rushes over to my car and tosses the bag into the backseat. Then, she takes Zoe from me and sits in the front seat. As soon as

I'm seated and the engine fires up, the reality begins to sink in.

They're here.

I have them.

My first instinct is to call Melody. She doesn't know she has a granddaughter. The fact I want to call her should be alarming, but it's not. Not after spending the last year leaning on this woman for emotional support under the thin veil of questioning her on the whereabouts of my wife.

"Hurry," Talia says. "I didn't make it very far last time."

Despite her words, I don't gun it like I normally would. The baby doesn't have a seat. I finally understand the term precious cargo.

"You escaped?"

"Today," she breathes. "Finally. But he caught me." A pained sound rattles from her. "I shot someone, Kostas. I was protecting me and Zoe. H-He's dead. I'm sorry, but I'd do it again and again to protect her."

Reaching over, I give her thigh a squeeze. "I don't know what the hell has been happening right under my goddamn nose, but I want you to tell me everything." I shoot her a hard look. "And don't ever apologize for protecting our little girl."

Our little girl.

I'm in fucking awe right now.

A dad. I'm a dad.

And I have my wife back.

chapter
ten

Talia

FOR THE FIRST TIME IN OVER A YEAR, I CAN FINALLY take a deep breath of relief. Oxygen can enter my lungs without a lump the size of a boulder blocking my airway.

Because Kostas is here.

He didn't give up on me, and he found me and Zoe, and we're finally safe.

Thunder booms and lightning strikes, lighting up the entire sky. The clouds open above us, and rain begins to pelt the windshield. It almost feels metaphorical, as if the rain is washing away every bad moment from this past year, hydrating the life back into us. For the last year, I've felt dead inside, but now, with Kostas here, I feel like my body is finally thriving once again. I was struggling to make it through each day, pieces of me slowly dying, but now I'm alive and can breathe easy.

Zoe's head lands on my shoulder, her body snuggling into my chest. When she babbles softly, Kostas glances over at the two of us, and for a brief moment our eyes meet. His hazel eyes tell me everything I need to know. Everything is going to be okay. He's going to make sure of it.

"When we get home, you're going to tell me everything that's happened," he says.

But my thoughts are stuck on one word. *Home.*

We're going home. Where we belong. Where we should've been this entire time.

And then it hits me. Home is the Pérasma Hotel. The hotel Aris part owns.

"We can't go back there." I sit up straight, and Zoe whines. It's late and she's exhausted. "Please, Kostas. We have to go somewhere else. Somewhere far away." My blood pressure is rising, and my heart is thumping against my ribcage.

"*Moró mou*, calm down." Kostas squeezes my thigh.

"Don't tell me to calm down, please." I'm working myself up. My head is feeling fuzzy, and it's hard to breathe again. "I can't risk Aris getting to Zoe and me again."

Kostas pulls into the parking garage, swings the car into his spot, and slams on the brakes. "Nobody is fucking taking you again. They're not going to live to have a chance."

Kostas pulls his phone out of his pocket and dials a number. Because we're still in the car, it rings over Bluetooth.

"Boss," Adrian says, answering on the first ring.

"I found Talia," Kostas says. "At Aris's house."

"Fuck."

"He and his bitch were holding her and my daughter captive."

Adrian curses under his breath again, but doesn't question anything Kostas is saying.

"I need you to go there and get *both* of them. Bring them to the cellar. Call me when it's done."

"Yes, sir."

Kostas hangs up, and after grabbing the bag I packed for Zoe, walks around and opens my door for me.

When we enter the villa, it's as if time has stopped. Everything is the same as it was the last time I was here. My flip-flops are still by the door where I left them. My favorite blanket to cuddle with is still thrown over the back of the couch. My school papers I left on the table in the foyer are still in the same spot. My purse I left in the bathroom when Aris took me is under the table. Kostas must've found it.

When I walk into our bedroom, one side of the bed is made. *Kostas's side.* The other side is how I left it. Messy sheets thrown about because I was in a rush to get to rehearsal that morning. My robe is still draped over the sitting chair. My pajamas are still on the floor next to the hamper because I missed when I tried to throw them in and told myself I would pick them up when I got home.

Only I never came home.

Because I was taken.

Because Aris fucking took me.

Took a year of my life.

"Kostas," I begin, in shock. "Did you live here while I was gone?"

His eyes meet mine, and with one look, I can feel everything he doesn't need to say. Pain. Loss. Confusion. Relief. I assess his features. There are dark circles under his gorgeous, glassy eyes. He's still as beautiful and captivating as he was a year ago, but he looks exhausted. Like he hasn't slept since I was taken.

"I couldn't do it," he admits, stepping toward me. Zoe's head is back on my shoulder. When she's nervous, she snuggles into me. And this is the first time she's ever been away from the only place she knows as home, so she's nervous.

Gently, Kostas rubs the top of Zoe's head and gives it a kiss before he leans over her and kisses my forehead as well. The sweet action has me momentarily closing my eyes, relishing in his touch. My body thrums, needing more of him.

"I looked for you every fucking day, *zoí mou*," he says softly. "At first, I was too pissed to sleep in here. I thought you ran. So I slept in the guest room. Then every day I searched, the signs pointed to you more than likely having been taken. I looked everywhere. I didn't think I left a single stone unturned." He curses under his breath. "I didn't even think to look in my brother's house." His jaw clenches in fury. "Fuck, he's been helping me look for you." He rubs his knuckles down the side of my cheek, his hand trembling with rage. "I couldn't bring myself to sleep in here. To move anything of yours. It would mean accepting you might not ever be back. I told myself once I got you back I would sleep in here again with you."

Be still, my heart.

This man. So powerful and controlling and cold. Shows zero mercy for anybody he comes across. And he couldn't sleep in our bed without me.

"Every day Aris would come home from work and tell me things about you. That you were a drunk and you stopped caring. That you had moved on. I didn't believe him, Kostas." Tears leak from my eyes. I'm finally here. Back in my home. With my husband. "I knew you would find me."

"It took me a fucking year, *zoí mou*. I failed you and our daughter."

"No, don't say that. You found us." He can't blame himself for this. The guilt will eat him up inside. I need my strong Kostas.

"After you put Zoe to bed, you're going to tell me every fucking thing my *brother* did to you and our daughter, every lie *he* told you, and I can promise you, I will make him regret every single goddamn thing he did and said."

If words weren't so matter-of-fact, the steely look in his eyes would tell me he means exactly what he says. When he finds Aris, he's not going to quickly kill him. He's going to slowly torture him for every day he held me prisoner, every lie he told me, and the thought has me almost smiling.

"I want to be there," I tell him. "I want to see Aris and Selene get what's coming to them."

Kostas grins. "Fuck, I've missed you." He gives me a chaste kiss on my lips.

Zoe stirs in my arms and it reminds me… "I don't have anywhere to lay her down." I glance at the bed. I suppose I could lay her in the center and line pillows along each side…

Kostas, of course, is already calling someone. "Thomas, this is Kostas Demetriou. I need a portable crib brought to my villa right away." He hangs up, and one side of his lips tip into a playful smirk. "The perks of owning and living in a hotel."

While I'm feeding Zoe, Kostas makes several phone calls in the other room. He's barking orders left and right, cursing and making threats like the mob boss he is, and my heart tugs in my chest. You don't realize how much you love your life until it's taken from you. And this life, the one with Kostas yelling at people, while our daughter snuggles in my arms, is all I want.

"What the fuck do you mean?" My body stills at his words and tone. Something is wrong.

Zoe knocks the bottle out of the way and climbs up

into my lap. Kostas enters the room and points to the sitting room attached to our bedroom for the gentleman to set up the crib. He quickly rolls it in, pops it open, and scurries out.

"Let me tell you something, my fucking wife was locked in that fucking house for the past goddamn year. Are you telling me you had no idea?"

"Kostas, who is that?" He shoots a glare my way and I give him one right back. At one time, his glare would've scared me, but now, it only turns me on. "Kostas." He ignore me, which pisses me off. I understand he's mad, but I am too. I was the one taken. "Kostas!"

"It's Basil," he barks out. "They got to the house and they're gone." The blood running through my veins goes cold. My eyes dart around us, and I find myself hugging Zoe tighter. They got away. Kostas wanted to take them out right then and there and I begged him to get us to safety first. And now they're missing. They can be anywhere. On their way here…

Kostas puts him on speakerphone. "Go ahead, Basil. Tell my wife how you were assigned to watch over that house and you never managed to find out she was in there."

"Boss, I swear," Basil sputters. "I never saw anything out of the ordinary. They came and went like everything was normal."

"Kostas, there's no way he would know," I tell him. "I was never allowed to leave the house. I even gave birth there." At my words, Kostas's eyes go to our daughter, and they soften slightly. "Unless Basil was able to get inside, he couldn't have seen me. Aris even had Selene drive across town to buy Zoe's stuff. I didn't even know that guy…Estevan, the one you shot his dick off, was guarding the place."

At my words, Kostas roars, "What in the actual fuck. Did you hear her?" he barks at his men. "Estevan was there?" he asks me, needing me to confirm.

"I heard her," Adrian says. "We'll find him."

"He's the guy I shot," I admit. "Several times. And then Aris finished him off. He's dead."

"Jesus fucking Christ," Kostas growls. He scrubs one of his hands over his face in frustration.

"Several of their drawers are empty," Adrian speaks. "And stuff is missing from the closet."

"They took both vehicles," Basil adds. "They're gone."

"Dammit." Kostas punches a hole in the drywall. Zoe jumps and starts crying. "Shit, I'm sorry." He gives her a pleading look, trying to convey how sorry he is.

She snuggles her face into the crook of my neck. "It's okay. She just doesn't know you yet." My words aren't meant to hurt him, but I can see it in his eyes how much they do.

"Adrian, you still there?" he growls.

"Yeah, Boss."

"Call the Minister of Public Order. Tell him I've found my wife and it was Aris and his cunt girlfriend who took her. I want every goddamn man searching for them. Every fucking available badge. They couldn't have gotten far," he barks out before he hangs up.

While I change Zoe's diaper and get her ready for bed, I can feel Kostas's eyes on us. I double-check the locks on the windows in the bedroom. With Aris and Selene missing, I'm scared they're going to show up here.

"Nobody is getting in here," Kostas vows.

"I know. I just need to make sure."

Once Zoe is comfortable in her temporary bed, with her pacifier in her mouth, her eyes roll back in her head. I laugh softly at how fast my baby girl falls asleep, and Kostas smiles.

"We made her," I tell him.

"She's perfect."

"That's because she's the best part of us."

"Let's talk." Taking my hand in his, Kostas leads me out to the living room. I glance back at the bedroom, but Kostas squeezes my hand, telling me it's okay.

When he sits on the sofa, I stay standing, needing to double-check the rest of the locks myself. Kostas watches as I go from the front door to each window, unlocking and re-locking every lock. "I'm scared, Kostas," I tell him once I'm done, sitting on the sofa next to him. "They could be any-where, planning their next move, and Aris thinks Zoe is his daughter."

"Why the fuck would he think that?" Kostas barks. Huh? Oh, shit! There's only one reason a man would think a baby is his. "You two had sex? When?" His eyes burn into mine. "While you were living under my roof? Fucking me? You were also fucking my brother?" Kostas tries to stand, but I grab his arms to tug him back down and climb into his lap, needing to be close to him. I can't let him push me away. I only just got him back. "What the fuck, Talia."

"Stop yelling, please," I beg, glancing back at the bed-room. "You're going to wake up Zoe." My hands frame his face. He hasn't shaved in some time, so his cheeks are all stubbly just the way I like it.

"I don't give a fuck," he says, but I know he does because his voice is now several notches lower than it was a minute ago. "Tell me why the fuck my brother, even for a second, would believe our daughter is his. Did you fuck him, Talia?" His eyes plead for me to tell him no, but I can't lie to him. It's time for the truth to come out. Maybe if I had told him the truth from the beginning, Aris never would've had a chance to take me.

"Kostas…" My heart is pounding like a drum in my chest.

"It's a yes or no. Tell me. Did. You. Fuck. My. Goddamn. Brother?"

I need to explain, but he's not giving me a chance to. "Kostas, please just let me explain," I beg. "It's not that simple."

"Yes or no!" he roars.

"Yes!" I blurt out, "Yes, I had sex with your brother."

chapter
eleven

Kostas

HER WORDS CHILL ME TO THE BONE. BUT THEY'RE wrong. The words don't match the pain in her eyes. Despite the rage thrashing at me, I can't unleash it. Talia is here. Straddling my thighs. Imploring me to understand.

I reach up and grip her delicate neck. Her bottom lip trembles as a tear races down her cheek. Tightening my hold, I draw her close to me until our lips nearly touch. I almost kiss her but pull away, hardening my glare.

"Take off your shirt and show me what he touched that's mine," I growl.

She stares at me for a long moment before grabbing the hem of her shirt and pulling it away. Her tits are full and nearly spilling from her plain black bra. I give her a nod to continue. She unhooks the bra, freeing her perfect breasts. The nipples are peaked and a lovely rosy color. I want to suck them until they're an angry shade of red.

"Did he touch you here?" I ask, cupping her breasts and running my thumbs along her nipples.

Another tear races down, dripping from her jaw. "I don't remember."

"One time?"

She gives me a clipped nod.

That. Motherfucker.

"It was your first time." I can barely contain the hate surging through my veins, burning just under my flesh begging to blaze.

"Kostas," she chokes out. "My first time was with you." More tears leak out. "You told me that. I need to believe that."

I close my eyes.

He raped her. He fucking raped her.

Before our honeymoon at some point. This whole time I thought it was some asshole she dated. Not my own goddamn brother.

"H-He, uh, he was d-devastated after your mom k-killed herself. Y-You were gone and I w-wanted to help. I went to check on him." A sob escapes her. "He was c-crying and I was crying. And...and..."

I open my eyes and slide my hands to her hips. "And..."

"I had t-to get the b-blood off him," she sobs, trembling. Her hands frantically cup my face. "I had t-to help him."

Sweet, innocent fucking Talia.

"Kostas, don't hate me." Her face crumples. My heart crushes.

I hastily swipe away something wet on my cheek. The ache that settles in my muscles dulls the fury. He hurt her. He hurt my fucking wife.

"Kostas," she whimpers.

I grip her throat again and pull her close. Our lips brush against the other. "Tell me all of it."

Her fingers slide into my hair as she steals a kiss. Soft. Sweet. Apologetic.

I hate it. I hate the apology in her kiss. It's dirty and wrong.

"Tell me," I whisper. "Talia, fucking tell me."

She needs to say it and I need to hear it.

"I was worried about him," she whines. "And then…I don't remember how it happened. He was j-just on me. K-Kissing me. The towel was g-gone and…"

Her body wracks with sobs. My fingers trace over her ribs and then my palms slide to her back, pulling her closer. She rests her forehead against mine. Salty tears fall on my face, mixing with my own.

He broke her.

He broke my fucking Talia.

And in doing so, he broke me.

"Tell me," I plead. I need her to say the words. To hand me the proverbial sword. I need to destroy and wage war. I need blood. I need fucking vengeance.

"He was so strong," she breathes. "I was scared."

Her lips press to mine, attempting to distract me. I nip at her bottom lip in warning.

No distractions. No more lies.

I need the truth.

"And then…and then he forced his way in." She sucks in a sharp breath before breaking down. "It hurt s-so bad, K-Kostas. I hated it. I was scared you would hate me."

I grip her jaw and kiss her hard before pulling away. Our eyes lock. Intense. Vicious. Feral.

"I could never hate you. I love you, goddammit," I growl, enunciating every word. "I love you so much it's killing me to hear this."

"I wanted to tell you," she whimpers. "But he said you'd kill me."

My chest feels like she cracked it open, shoved her hands inside, and scooped out my fucking soul.

"Talia…" My voice is low and deadly. I need her to understand me. "I would never fucking hurt you. Ever. Even if you slept with the motherfucker of your own free will. Fucking. Never. Don't you see? I'm under your goddamn spell. You got inside me. It was so fucking dark and, Jesus, Talia, you were all light. I wanted that light so bad I could taste it." I kiss her supple lips. "I'd never hurt you. Do you hear me? Never."

Her kiss is frantic—thankful and desperate—as she claws at my tie. I rip her pants roughly down her ass as she sits up to aid in my effort. We're both clumsy and overly eager as we yank off our offending clothes that stand between us. I manage to get my jacket and tie off by the time she pulls away her pants and underwear. She works on my slacks as I pull hard on my shirt, and the buttons go flying. As soon as my cock is free in her hot, soft hand, I grab her hips, pulling her to me. My hand wraps around hers to hold my cock as she slides down over my length. With a hard thrust, I drive into her from beneath her. We both groan in unison.

"Kostas," she cries out. "I missed you."

Our lips crash together as her fingers claw at my bare skin on my chest. She pushes the fabric down over my shoulders so she can dig her nails there too. My fingertips bite into her hip as I guide her to fuck me rough and fast. Being inside her is the best fucking feeling in the world.

Sliding my free hand between us, I find her clit to offer her some quick pleasure. I won't last long. Not after a year of celibacy. I'm going to come like a teenage boy. Soon.

Her pussy clenches around me when I rub her clit in firm, rough circles. I hiss in pleasure, spiking my hips up harder. She bites on my lip and rakes her nails down over my pectorals.

"Fucking come, Talia," I bark out. "I need you to come before I embarrass myself in front of my wife."

She smiles against my lips and rocks her hips in unison with the way I rub her. When sweet whines begin climbing out of her throat, I know she's finding ecstasy with me. I pinch her clit in the way she used to love and am rewarded with a full-bodied shudder. My name screeches past her lips as she comes wildly. The frantic, feral way in which she does it is enough to send me over the edge. I lean forward and suck on her neck hard enough to mark her as my nuts seize up. Grinding up into her, I groan as I flood her with a year's worth of pent-up release.

Her arms circle around my neck as she hugs me to her. I bury my nose against her flesh, inhaling her sweaty, unique scent. I lick her salty skin and brand her with my teeth. I'm already hardening again like I'm fifteen years younger.

Fuck.

She does this to me.

I stand with her in my arms and kick out of my slacks and shoes. She holds on, worshipping me with her kisses as I carry us to our bed so I can return the favor. We fall into the bed—where we fucking belong—and I kiss her deeply. She helps me rip my shirt off the rest of the way and then I'm driving into her slowly, my eyes glued to hers.

I want to see her.

I want to look at her for-fucking-ever.

We spend hours tasting and teasing and fucking. I

can't keep my dick out of her. We're sweaty and messy and fucking exhausted. And yet, we can't part ways. It isn't until we've showered and I'm about to bend her over the bed again that we're dragged from our sex-fest haze.

"Da-da-da-da-da."

The baby babbling in the other room warms me to my soul.

"I'll get her," I grunt as I yank on some boxers. Talia grabs one of my T-shirts from the drawer to wear as I leave to get our baby.

When I turn on the light, Zoe watches me with wide blue eyes. Fuck, she's so damn perfect. I stalk over to her and pluck her from the crib. Hugging her to me, I inhale her hair.

"I love you, *agapiménos*," I whisper. "I will kill that motherfucker for stealing you and your mother from me."

I consider telling her all the horrible ways I will torture that monster, but then I figure that's not a fatherly thing to do. It's something *my* father would do. And I'm not him.

Carrying her back to the room, I can't help but smile when I see Talia cozied up in our bed. She's so fucking beautiful with her hair wet and messy. Her lips raw from kissing. Purple bruises from my mouth littering her skin.

I settle on the bed and adjust the little one so she's nestled between us. On my side with my arm propped under my head, I admire the cute as fuck kid we made. Talia mimics my position and smiles proudly at our daughter.

Aris—my goddamn brother—took from me.

Took and took and took.

Never again.

As soon as I find him, *and I will find him*, I'm going to take from him.

Skin. Hair. Teeth. Organs.

I'm going to take from him until there's nothing left to take.

A slap to my face erases all murderous thoughts. The little angel with the blue eyes and brown hair swats at me again as though she's trying to touch me. Leaning in, I let her abuse me. She's vicious as she grabs a handful of scruff and tries to pull me to her mouth.

"She's hungry?" I ask because I know fuck all about babies.

"She's been teething, so it could be that. Or she's curious. Usually she cries when she's hungry."

"What do I do?" I grunt. "Fuck, she has a good grip."

Talia laughs and untangles the tiny fingers clawing at me. "For one, don't offer your face as a chew toy."

Zoe's face pinches and she lets out a pouty cry.

"But she likes it," I argue.

"She also likes hair and blankets and shirts."

I grin down at my baby. "Don't listen to Mommy. You can eat my face if it makes you happy."

Zoe coos and wriggles more, attempting to grab at me. I offer her my thumb and she sets to trying to pull it to her mouth.

"I'll make her a bottle," Talia says with a laugh.

While she's gone, I stare at my perfect daughter. How is it this afternoon I was wallowing in despair and murdering my fucking father with my mother's pillow and hours later I have my wife back and a daughter I never knew about? I feel like I'll blink awake and this will be some cruel as fuck dream.

The baby swats at me with her other hand.

"You're distracting like your mother," I grumble but smile at her.

Talia walks in, messy hair, perfect nipples poking through the thin shirt, and bare legs on display, carrying a fucking bottle.

"Distracting," I whisper to Zoe. "You're both bad news for the bad guy."

Talia grins as she hands me the bottle and climbs onto the bed, flashing me her naked pussy beneath her shirt. "Out there you're the bad guy. In here, you're Daddy." She leans in and kisses me. "And spoiler alert, he's the good guy."

chapter
twelve

Talia

THE SOUND OF MY DAUGHTER BABBLING HAPPILY from beside me wakes me from my deep slumber. I open my eyes and find Zoe lying on her back, her feet in the air, and her fists in her mouth. Kostas's side of the bed is empty, but in his place are a dozen pillows entrapping Zoe. I laugh, imagining him building a barricade to keep her safe in the bed. He doesn't know she's fully crawling and could climb right over that wall if she wanted to.

"You're awake." Kostas walks through the door, freshly showered and shaved, dressed in his power suit. God, he's so sexy. Zoe spots him, and wanting off the bed, turns over on her belly and crawls toward him. Kostas's eyes widen, and I laugh.

"Yeah, she can crawl." I nod toward the makeshift wall. "That wouldn't stop her, but that was a good try." I stretch my arms over my head. For the first time in over a year, I feel well rested. It's been too long since I've felt safe enough to get a good night's sleep. "I slept so well," I tell Kostas. His lips curl into a boyish grin.

"I did too."

"I missed this bed," I joke, and he laughs good-naturedly.

"Is that all you missed?"

"No," I admit, "I missed lying next to you… Too bad when I woke up you were gone." I pout playfully.

"I've had a busy morning," he says, picking Zoe up. She reaches for his scruff, but it's gone, so instead she pats the sides of his face.

"Any news?" I sit up, suddenly remembering that this feeling of safety and comfort is only an illusion.

"Not yet," Kostas says. "But I've removed Aris's name from all the accounts, so other than his personal account, which he can't use without leaving a trail, he has zero access to any of the Demetriou funds." He glances down at Zoe, who is chewing on her fist again.

"She's hungry." I climb out of bed to grab a bottle for her. When I'm done making it, I take Zoe from Kostas and sit in the chair near the window to feed her. "What does your dad have to say about all of this?" I know he's not a fan of me. He used me to get back at my dad for having an affair with his wife, but it backfired when Kostas and my marriage became real.

"My dad is dead and he left me in charge of the organization. He no longer has a say."

My eyes fly to meet Kostas's, but he's not looking at me. He's standing in the same place, glancing down at his phone nonchalantly, like he didn't just tell me his father is dead.

"What?" I ask in shock. "Your dad is dead?" When he doesn't look up, I say, "Kostas, look at me." His eyes lift from his phone. "Stop what you're doing for two damn seconds. Since when is your father dead? Aris never mentioned that. He would've mentioned it. Did he know?"

Kostas tucks his phone into his pocket, finally giving me his undivided attention. I can hear his phone vibrating from over here, but he ignores it. "You almost sound like you care about how Aris might feel…"

"Don't go there." I shoot him a glare. "It's just the last year, every time Aris would go on one of his rants, if it wasn't about you, it was about your father. He was obsessed with bringing him down. When he finds out he's dead, he's going to lose it." Instinctually, my eyes graze the room. If he can't focus on destroying his father anymore, his entire attention will be on destroying his brother.

"He's not going to touch you," Kostas growls. "I'm going to kill him, just like I killed my father. Only, unlike Father's death, which was quick and painless, Aris's is going to be drawn out. He's going to feel every ounce of fucking pain we felt this past year from him taking you and our daughter."

Oh, shit! *He* killed his father? What the hell happened while I was gone? "You killed him?" It should worry me that I'm more shocked than upset that my husband killed his own father, but it doesn't. I know Kostas, and if he killed his dad, there was a reason why. My husband might be cold and cruel when he needs to be, but he's also smart and calculating. Everything he does is for a reason.

"Turns out he and my brother have far more in common than anybody thought. He was cheating on my mom for years before she had her affair with your dad. And Aris knew the entire time." He scrubs his hand along the side of his face in frustration. "He instilled loyalty into us from the time we were born, but he was anything but loyal to his own wife. I walked in on him yesterday getting fucked by some whore in the bed my mother slept in, so I made sure the last breath he ever took was in that same bed."

Yesterday… "That was why you were at Aris's. To let him know your father is dead."

"He invited me to his house a million times over the last year, but I always declined. Didn't care to hang out with him and his skank. But I felt I owed it to him to tell him in person. Showed up unannounced and that's how I found you. I saw you looking out the window. Thought I lost my fucking mind." Wow, the death of his father was what led Kostas to finding me. Had he not killed him, he may not have ever found us. No, I refuse to believe that. It was only a matter of time.

"I'm glad you killed him," I blurt out, and Kostas grins. "Because it meant finding us," I explain.

"I would've found you," Kostas says, his tone filled with conviction. "But yes, I suppose his death was meant to be."

Zoe finishes her bottle and bats it away, sitting up and then crawling off the chair and onto the floor. When she gets to Kostas's shiny expensive shoes, she scratches her tiny nails along them, curiously. Kostas picks her up and gives her a kiss on her cheek, and my heart warms. This is all I ever wanted, and now we're so close to having it. All that's in our way is Aris and Selene still on the run.

"It's Aris's entire purpose to make you and your father pay," I tell him, remembering all the times Aris told me how much he despises them.

"He can try." Kostas shrugs, as if my words barely deserve acknowledgment. "But now he has limited resources to do so. It won't matter anyway because I have every man out there searching for him. We'll find him soon."

"Like you found Niles?" I accuse. I shouldn't poke the hornet's nest, but I can't help it. He's so sure he's going to find Aris, yet my father has been underground for even longer and he still hasn't been found.

Kostas glares. "I don't give a fuck about finding Niles. He's a waste of air. Your brother has taken over and is turning a nice profit. But finding Aris will happen, and when I do he will regret ever fucking with what's mine." He gives Zoe another kiss on the top of her head.

"And until you do? What if it takes months or even years? Are Zoe and I going to be held captive here as well?" If my dad was able to hide out, I can't even imagine what Aris is capable of.

Kostas glances over at me. "You will never be held captive again. I have men surrounding the villa, and if you want to go somewhere, we go. I'll make sure you're safe."

"I'd like to take Zoe to the beach." I stand and walk over to them. Her gaze flits over to me and she leans toward me, so I can take her. "Every day I was stuck in his house, I would watch the waves and wish I were back down here. We spent a lot of time at the pool, but it wasn't the same. There were walls holding us in. I want Zoe to feel the sand between her toes. To feel the waves hit her body. I want her to know what it's like to be free, even if she's too young to understand it."

"Then to the beach we'll go. But first, you need to call your mother and brother. They've been almost as worried about you as I was." Kostas pulls his phone out of his pocket and hands it to me.

Wow, things have changed. Kostas is telling me to call my family… "Have you spoken to them?" I ask, taking the phone from him.

"Your mother and I speak almost every day," he says. "I guess you can say we formed a sort of truce. We both wanted to find you. And your brother is nothing like your father. He actually handles business the way it should be handled."

"Thank you." I bring myself up on my tiptoes and give Kostas a kiss.

"For what?"

"For finding and saving us." I give him another kiss. "For loving us."

After calling my mom, who cries when she finds out I'm safe, then cries even harder when she finds out she's a grandma, then tells me she's coming to visit, and Phoenix, who—without the tears—also promises to visit soon, Kostas, Zoe, and I head down to the beach. Since Zoe doesn't have a suit, we grab one from the hotel store.

I notice a few men following us, and Kostas notes they're our guards. I still can't help but glance around. Maybe this wasn't a good idea after all. But I still keep walking toward the beach. After a year of being held prisoner, I think I just need a moment to feel free.

Kostas has one of the cabana boys set up lounge chairs and umbrellas for us. I throw a blanket down, and Kostas sets Zoe down on it. We watch as she crawls to the end and reaches for the sand. She fists a handful and is bringing it up to her mouth when Kostas swoops in and saves her.

"No, no, *agapiménos*," he says softly. "That will taste bad."

Zoe's face scrunches up in confusion, and Kostas laughs. It sounds so carefree, so unlike Kostas. Being a father really does bring out the best in him. All she has to do is look at him and he transforms from hard to soft. "So curious, just like your mother." He taps her nose with his finger and she giggles.

Grabbing his phone from the blanket where he tossed it along with his shirt, I open the camera and take a photo of the two of them. When Kostas leans in and kisses her cheek, I snap another one.

I don't realize I'm crying until Kostas looks over at me and frowns. "What's the matter?"

"Nothing." I wipe the falling tears. "Everything is perfect." I step toward the two people who are my entire world. "Every day when I was stuck in that house, I would imagine what it would be like when you found us. But my imagination didn't do it justice. Getting to see you hold our daughter in person is better than anything I ever dreamed of."

When I click on the photos I just took, I notice a tattoo I didn't see before. Glancing from the phone to Kostas, I spot it on the side of his ribcage. "That's new," I point out. Dropping the phone onto the blanket, I step toward him and bend so I can get a better look at it.

"I got it a few months after you disappeared," he says. The tattoo is of a grenade, cracked open at the seams, and inside of it are bright red beads…no, not beads. Seeds. From a pomegranate. "I thought you left me," he admits, and I stand back up.

"What?"

"We were fighting that morning and then you disappeared. I thought you left me."

I glance back down at the tattoo. I'm almost positive the seeds symbolize Proserpina—me—being forced to stay in the Underground, but… "What does the grenade mean?"

"My world being blown apart." Kostas swallows thickly. "The day you went missing my entire world exploded." And just like that, I fall even deeper in love with my husband.

The day is spent playing in the sand and swimming in the ocean. We order lunch to be brought down, and only when Zoe is so exhausted, she can't keep her eyes open, do we go back up to our villa.

After laying her down in the new crib—yes, while we

were at the beach, my crazy husband somehow had an entire nursery of furniture brought in—I find Kostas on the phone in his office. It reminds me of the time he fucked me on his desk, and that thought has me wanting him to take me there again. We've lost so much time together. All I want is to spend all my time with him. Create new memories to push away every memory that was created this past year.

When he spots me in the doorway, he abruptly ends his phone call.

"That was rude," I joke. "Won't whoever you were talking to wonder why you hung up on him?" I saunter over to him and he spreads his muscular thighs to let me in. He's still in his swim trunk sans shirt, and I take a moment to memorize every hard ridge, every tattoo on his body, including the tattoo he got while I was gone.

"I'm the boss," he says, running his hands up the sides of my hips. "I answer to no one."

"Do you answer to me?" I ask, my voice flirty.

His fingers find my pebbled nipples through my thin bathing suit top and he pinches them roughly. Waves of pleasure shoot through my entire body.

Kostas lifts me up and sets me on his desk. Papers crinkle under my weight, but he doesn't seem to care. "You and me aren't business," he says, pushing the material aside. He leans in and wraps his lips around my nipple, and the coolness of his breath sends a shiver straight down my spine. "But yes, *zoí mou*, I answer to you." He bites down on my nipple, then darts his tongue out to lick it, as he continues to pinch and pull at the other one. When I let out a low moan, tugging on his messy hair, he glances up at me with a wicked smirk. "I may not know a lot about this whole marriage thing, but I do know one thing…"

He pulls my bottoms down my legs, dropping them onto the floor, and I spread my legs so I'm completely exposed to him. "What's that?" I prompt, needing him to get to his point before I lose all my focus.

"Any smart man knows his wife is in charge." With his hands pushed against my thighs to keep me open, he dips his face down and swipes his tongue up my center.

"You're wrong," I tell him through a moan. He sucks my clit into his mouth and bites down playfully. "You do know a lot…" Kostas pushes two fingers into me, and I arch my back, craving more. Always more. "You're a really good husband…" I breathe. He adds another finger, stroking my insides in a way that has me squirming in pleasure. With every touch, every lick, every stroke, he works my entire body into a frenzy, until I'm coming all over his face and fingers, screaming his name.

"You only think I'm a good husband because I make you come." He smirks playfully as he stands and pushes his swim trunks down. I can't help but laugh. I love when my husband is playful.

"That's not the only reason." I reach forward and grip his hard cock. It doesn't need any preamble, but I stroke it a few times just because I want to.

Kostas watches for a few seconds before he loses his patience. With my hand still gripping his shaft, he steps closer, allowing me to guide him inside of me. As he slowly enters me, his thick, long length stretches me until he's buried to the hilt. "Fuck, *moró mou.*" He groans. "I've missed your sweet cunt so fucking much." His hands land on either side of me, and with his strong arms caging me in, he fucks me hard and deep.

His mouth finds my neck and he suckles on my flesh. I

can smell myself on his breath, and it sends me over the edge once again. Kostas's head lifts, and his eyes meet mine. "I'm never letting you out of my sight again," he vows. And with one last thrust, he finds his own release.

His movements still momentarily, and then he pulls out. Glancing down, I spot his cum dripping out of me and onto the desk. "Kostas," I breathe. We were too wrapped up in each other last night, and then again just now… "I'm not on birth control."

Kostas smirks, his gaze focused on the mess that's now dripping onto the floor. I try to close my legs, but he grips my knees, forcing them to remain open. He swipes at the liquid, gathering it onto his fingers, then smears his cum along the hood of my clit, as if he's claiming me all over again. The thought has my insides clenching in need. "Kostas," I repeat breathily. "I could get pregnant…"

"That's good, *moró mou*," he says, looking me dead in the eyes. "Because I intend to knock you up again as soon as fucking possible."

chapter
thirteen

Kostas

I FLICK THROUGH THE SCREENS OF THE VARIOUS cameras on my app. My newest obsession. Nothing. Nothing is better than something. It's been nearly a week since I got Talia and Zoe home, but we're on edge. Not Zoe, of course. She's cute as fuck and learning the lay of the villa. I didn't know babies could be so goddamn fast. I've been tempted to build her a little cage to keep her safe from furniture and decorations and tiny things she seems to find on the floor to put into her mouth. Talia says no to cages.

My phone rings, and I answer Adrian's call on the first ring.

"Anything?" I grunt out. I swivel around in my chair to glower at the rain. My beach babies are restless stuck inside. Thank God Melody and Stefano showed up yesterday. Otherwise, I'd never get any work done. Now, they can visit and catch up with Talia while I hunt down the motherfuckers who hurt her.

"There's some chatter…"

I stand abruptly, nearly crushing my phone to my ear. "Spill, Adrian."

"With Estevan's body turning up, his people are pissed. They're not loyal to Aris like Estevan was. Estevan kept them in check because Aris's dime insured that. Now that he's gone, the roaches have scattered. Basil and Bronn have been following one of his men named Gutter."

"Gutter?"

He snorts. "Rats. Roaches. They're all pieces of shit. Anyway, Gutter seems to be planning something. Rallying his troops."

"To do what?"

"Not sure. I've been fed information that maybe they're waiting for you to fly out to Thessaloniki again. Might try to take out the private jet or put a hit on you while you're there."

"Why not here and now?"

"You're vulnerable there because you travel with minimal security. Here, at the hotel, it's a fuckin' fortress."

"Is Gutter calling the shots or is Aris still pulling strings? Aris is a sneaky sonofabitch."

"Aris is a ghost. But…"

"But what?"

"I got a tip about an older man who fits Niles's description staying about thirty minutes from here."

My entire body tenses. "What the fuck, Adrian? You could have led with that."

"It's just a tip. Nothing's confirmed. I was going to check it out. Didn't want to leave the king of the fortress unprotected."

I smirk. "The king can handle himself. Plus, security on the hotel is extra beefed. I'm about to head back to my family. Call me if you get Niles. Bring him to the cellar. Tell Basil and Bronn to keep me informed."

"Later, Boss."

We hang up and I stride through the hotel. It's pouring down rain and I hate to get out in it, but I miss my wife and our precious little angel. I grab one of the hotel umbrellas and pop it open as I step outside into the nasty weather. Wind hits hard from the west, soaking my slacks with rain. I grumble as I stalk along the pathways toward my villa. When I arrive, Melody and Stefano are just leaving.

"The weatherman said it's only supposed to get worse," Melody says in greeting. "Stefano and I are going to call it an early night. Maybe order room service. Breakfast tomorrow, though?"

"Pomegranate has an excellent brunch menu. We can meet there in the morning," I agree. "Stay dry."

Stefano holds the umbrella over her as she leans in and hugs me. I'm stiff as I accept her embrace.

"You two made a beautiful baby," she says. "Thank you for being such a wonderful husband to her. I knew you had it in you."

Stefano nods at me as she pulls away. Then, they disappear into the rain. Once on the front stoop of the villa, I close the umbrella and prop it against the wall. I mash in the code and then push through the door. It smells like coffee and Talia. Two warm, comforting scents.

I kick off my rain-soaked shoes and then walk through the villa on a hunt for them. I find Talia in Zoe's bathroom, running her a bath. Zoe splashes from her little seat inside the tub. With Talia's blond hair curtaining her face as she looks down at the little angel below her, I can't help but think she looks like an angel herself. *And Daddy is from the depths of the Underworld.* Somehow, our opposites attract. When she sees me, she grins, and her brilliant blue eyes glitter with love. It's a punch to the chest every time she knocks me over with her intensity. There's no questioning our feelings anymore.

"Someone is soaked," Talia says, smiling. "Why don't you go grab a hot shower and we'll eat after? I'll preheat the oven to cook a frozen lasagna once I'm done with her bath. It won't be homemade, but it's better than getting out in that weather."

I walk over to her and kiss the top of her head. I ruffle Zoe's dark hair. "I'll make it quick."

"Any news?"

"A lead on Niles. Maybe some other shit, but I won't know until Basil and Adrian check it out."

She purses her lips together. "Are we safe?"

"Of course."

Her brows pull together as though she doesn't believe me. It makes me bristle, but I don't let it get to me. After the hell she's gone through, she's allowed to have anxiety. One day, hopefully, it'll fade completely. I quickly shed my soaked clothes and breeze through a shower. Since we're not going anywhere, I pull on a pair of gray sweatpants, some socks, and a white T-shirt. Talia likes it when I'm dressed down. With my hair still wet and messy, I pad through the house to find her in the kitchen, Zoe propped on her hip.

"Here, hold her," she instructs.

I take my baby, who now smells sweet and clean, bouncing her in my arms as Talia peels the plastic film away from the lasagna and sits it on a tray. She then busies herself with making a salad while the oven preheats. Zoe and I walk over to the window where the storm seems to worsen.

Boom!

Thunder crashes loud and hard enough the windows rattle.

"That was intense," Talia exclaims from behind me. "This storm—"

Boom! Boom! Boom!

My blood runs cold. Thunder doesn't sound like that. It doesn't hit that quickly either. What the fuck?

"Get in the closet," I bark out, grabbing Talia's arm and rushing her through the villa as the booms continue.

"Kostas," she cries out. "What's happening?"

"We're being attacked."

"W-What?"

"Turn the lights off. Hide in the closet," I bellow as I grab my phone from the bedroom. I dial Adrian and he doesn't answer. When I call Basil, he picks up. "We're being fucking hit."

"We're five minutes out and I have Caymon on the other line. He says Aris's Porsche is at the front. Explosives are going off near the front entrance. Bold ass motherfucker," Basil huffs. "Want me to take him out, Boss?"

"No kill shot. He's mine. I want him in the cellar," I bark out.

Basil says something to Bronn and then grunts, "Bronn says Caymon's men have the Porsche surrounded."

"I'm on my way." I hang up and shove my phone into my pocket.

I stalk into the closet to find Talia and Zoe watching me with wide eyes. I shove my feet into a pair of tennis shoes and shove my suit jackets aside to get to my gun safe. After punching in the code, I pull out a Glock, check the magazine, and then hand the weapon to Talia.

"Shoot first, ask questions later," I hiss before turning to pull out my AR-15. "They have Aris's Porsche surrounded."

"Be careful," Talia cries out. "Please."

I rush over to her, planting a kiss on her lips and then one on Zoe's soft head. "Shoot anyone who walks through that closet, Talia. I have my phone. Call me if you need me. I'll be back as soon as we have that motherfucker detained."

As I leave, I turn off all the lights, to keep them safe under the cover of darkness. The doors are all locked and I slip out the front into the pouring rain. Wind violently whips at me, slashing me with rain and soaking me to the bone. I sprint through the downpour, racing toward the front of the hotel under the cover of shadows and between buildings. I'm not letting my guard down for an instant.

"Boss," Caymon hisses from between a building. He stumbles out, holding his side. "It's a fucking—"

His head explodes in front of me as he collapses to the dirt. I lift my AR and turn toward the direction the bullet came from. Spraying bullets into the trees, I try to mow down the attacker. This isn't Aris's style, which means he has his men doing his dirty work. Someone grunts from the trees and I charge after them.

I tackle the man and lay a hard punch to his kidney. He groans, attempting to roll away from me, splattering us with mud, but I'm stronger. I flip the man and shove the barrel of my AR against his Adam's apple, making him gag and cough.

Niles motherfucking Nikolaides.

The urge to shoot his head right off his spine is strong, but I need answers. I kick him hard in the stomach, making him howl.

"Get the fuck up and walk," I bellow.

He groans and unsteadily makes his way to his feet.

"Turn." As soon as his back is to me, I poke the gun in between his shoulder blades. "To your left." My phone buzzes and I quickly answer it. "What?"

"It's Adrian," he barks out. "Where are you?"

"Walking Niles to the goddamn cellar. Where are you?"

"Standing behind the Porsche. We can see them inside. A man and a woman. Call it and I'll put a bullet in their heads."

"No," I growl. "I want my brother alive. I'm going to tie down this fucker and then I'm on my way."

"Hold on," he bites at me as he talks to someone. "No fuckin' way. Basil has Phoenix."

That traitorous motherfucker.

"Tell Basil to bring Phoenix to the cellar to keep his daddy company and to watch them both. You keep Aris there."

We hang up just as I storm into the groundskeeper's house with Niles leading the way. The groundskeeper sits on the sofa, soaked to the bone, holding pressure to his stomach as blood blooms over his hands. He gurgles out something to me, but it's too late. Hot pain slices through the back of my arm, just as I'm turning. Whoever nearly stabbed me in the goddamn back, missed a deadlier hit when I moved at the last minute, but it still hurts like a motherfucker. With my gun still trained on Niles, I swing out with my leg, taking down my assailant. They hit the ground with a loud grunt.

I sling the AR to the guy's face and pop him right in the mouth with three bullets. Niles tries to run, but I crack him hard in the back of the head with the butt of the AR. He falls hard on his knees but doesn't go completely down.

"Get your ass down those stairs or I'll kick you down them," I roar, shoving the barrel into his back. "Move."

He groans and curses all the way down to the cellar. I

force him into the chair and tie him tight enough around his wrists, his hands turn purple. I'm about to head back upstairs when Basil and Bronn manhandle Phoenix down the steps. His face is beat all to hell, but he's raging like a beast. Not taking any chances, I stay until they get him subdued with an elbow to the face and tied down.

"I'll be back soon with my brother and his bitch. Don't let them go anywhere."

Basil and Bronn both nod as I take the steps up two at a time. My arm hurts like a motherfucker, but I'm high on adrenaline. I've thirsted for vengeance for what feels like forever. I'm finally getting it. Fucking finally.

I run through the rain toward the front gate with my AR raised and ready to fire. My staff are trained in the event we're ever attacked, so the guests should be fairly safe, although it's going to be a helluva PR nightmare. I'll have Josef pissed as fuck having to cover our shit, but there's nothing money won't buy—even the Minister of Public Order's compliance.

When the Porsche comes into view, flashes of light can be seen in conjunction with pops of gunfire. My men are shooting into the vehicle against my orders. What the fuck!

Racing toward them, I nearly mow down Adrian in the process.

"They shot him against direct orders—"

"Something isn't right, Boss!" Adrian barks out.

I shove past him toward the Porsche. Pushing a guy out of my way, I fling open the door. A man and a woman are slumped over, the entire interior splattered with their blood. The guy is an older man with his hands tied behind his back. The woman has gray hair and her arms are bound too.

Fuck.

Fuck.

Talia.

Bullets spray at me and I dive down into the mud, wincing at the pain searing through my hip where I've been clipped. The guy I'd pushed away splats beside me, his head blown off.

"Boss," Adrian calls out from nearby. "Stay the fuck down. I'm gonna get the bastard!"

Rolling onto my back, I wince when my arm screams in protest and my hip burns like a motherfucker. I strain my neck, searching for the shooter. The rain is relentless and it's dark as fuck. I work myself into a squat and rush around to the back of the car. Popping can be heard just north. I see Adrian's big form not far away. We make eye contact and I nod at him, pointing in the direction of the shooter.

We're coming for you, asshole.

And you're going to wish you'd never been fucking born.

chapter
fourteen

Talia

WITH ZOE CLINGING TO MY CHEST, I LISTEN TO the front door slam closed. Zoe, the six-month-old that she is, squirms, wanting to play in the closet. She doesn't understand what's going on, or that she was born into a world where the villains and monsters I read to her about, the ones who always get taken down by the white knights, are real, and they don't get taken down as easily in real life as they do in her books. Sometimes, in fact, they don't get taken down at all.

Once upon a time I thought Kostas was a monster. But now that I've seen Aris in action, I know the difference. Whereas Kostas is powerful and smart, and makes calculated decisions, Aris is cruel and vindictive, and makes decisions based on his emotions. His need for revenge. Kostas may not be like the knights in Zoe's books, but he's still *my* knight. And I know without a doubt my dark knight will do everything in his power to make sure his princesses are safe.

Where is he?

What's taking so long?

The booms we heard sounded like explosions. I pray Mom and Stefano are safe someplace. I should try to call and check on them, but not until Zoe and I are in the clear. Kostas would lose his mind if I left the closet to look for them. I have to trust my stepdad will take care of Mom.

Fear clings to me and I can't shake it off. An ominous feeling washes over me. I'm not safe here in this closet. Deep down, I know it's Aris. He can't let his brother win. It's all he's bitched about for a year. Destroying him. Toying with him. We're Kostas's weakness and Aris is smart enough to know that. He'll hunt us down. Nothing will satisfy him until he has us.

Over my dead body.

I'll shoot him in the face before I let him take us again.

I can't live as a captive ever again. I won't do that to Zoe.

"Ba-ba-ba," Zoe babbles around the pacifier I keep trying to push back into her mouth to keep her quiet. She's getting annoyed that I won't let her loose to play. In a few minutes, she's going to get frustrated and will soon be screaming her tiny little head off. My daughter doesn't do well with being confined. Hopefully, whatever is happening, will be over by then.

Hope is worthless at a time like this. My brain trumps the hope flittering in my heart. These people are mobsters, not normal men. That means hope is useless, unlike the gun beside me.

Feeling around in the dark, I find a shoe and try to hand it to Zoe to distract her. She takes it for a second before she drops it to the ground and wriggles, trying to get free.

"Ba-da-da," she babbles some more, frustration evident in her tone.

Come on, Kostas.

We don't like being alone without you.

"Shh, baby, let's go night-night." It's close to her bedtime, so maybe she will go with it. Lifting her into my arms, I start to rock her back and forth, when I hear something shatter. Zoe hears it too because her head, which was lying against my arm, pops up, smacking me in the face.

Crunch. Crunch. Crunch.

Footsteps on glass.

Oh, God.

Someone's in the house.

Grabbing the gun from beside me, I'm preparing to do as Kostas said—shoot first, ask questions later.

I strain my ears, hoping it's just the storm. But I can hear voices inside. Whispers. Something crashing to the floor. A door slams and more voices. The bedroom light turns on and shines in under the crack of the doors.

People are here.

They're going to find us.

My body trembles with fear and adrenaline courses through me. If we can be quiet, maybe they won't think to look in the closet.

"Ba!" Zoe screeches, and I wince. If someone is in here, Zoe's voice just gave us away.

"Shh," I whisper. "Shh, baby."

But she's not quiet and starts to screech as she squirms.

Come home, Kostas!

When the closet door swings open, momentarily blinding me with the new light shining in, I let out a choked sound of horror. I have no clue who is standing there, but if it were Kostas, he would've made his presence known. So, with Zoe wrapped tightly in one of my arms, I raise the gun with my other and shoot.

Bang. Bang. Bang.

Three shots go off, making my hand go numb and my ears ring.

My eyes adjust just in time to see Selene stumble back. I hit her somewhere based on her howling, but she's still alive.

"You fucking bitch," she screams, stalking toward me like one of those crazy zombies who can't be brought down. "You shot me!" Blood seeps from her lower abdomen and it's hard to tell if I got her good or just clipped her.

I aim again, hoping to hit her in the heart, and—

"It's over." Aris comes out of nowhere and tackles me. Still trying to hold Zoe in my arms, I hit and kick at him. But he's stronger and quickly disarms me, before pinning me to the floor. Zoe is flung out of my grip, and before I can grab her, Selene plucks her off the ground.

Blood curdling screams.

Zoe! My baby!

She's screaming for me and I need to get to her.

"No!" I wail. My drive to get to my daughter takes over, and grabbing the first thing I can get my hands on, I plow it into Aris's face. He's caught off guard long enough that I'm able to roll over and get out of his grip. I'm about to stand, so I can run after Zoe, when Aris tackles me from behind. With his weight on top of me, my arms give out, and my chin hits the hardwood floor. Something metallic swarms my mouth.

Zoe's screams go louder, spurring me to focus on her instead of the pain.

My baby. I need to get to her.

But before I can move forward, Aris's strong hands grip my biceps, and he flips me over onto my back, smashing the back of my head in the process. He crawls up my body, wrapping his legs around my torso. With him hovering above me, I can make out his features.

His eyes scream hate. Fury. Revenge. But the way he's smirking, it sends shivers down my spine. He's enjoying what's happening. Just as I thought he planned all of this, and he's confident enough to believe he's going to win.

Not if I can help it.

"Did you really think I would let you and that baby leave that easily?" He chuckles darkly.

"Fuck you!" I spit the blood that's been building up in my mouth in his face.

"Been there, done that." He cocks his hand back to hit me, but I see it coming. And lifting my butt into the air, I knee him in the back, forcing him to fall forward enough to lose his balance.

Taking advantage of his current state, I slide my body backward then knee him in the dick as hard as I can. He groans and rolls to his side, as I roll to mine, determined to get to my daughter. We're both on our feet, running out the bedroom door, when something heavy smacks me in the side of my face.

I fall forward, my face catching the side of the end table. Gray. Blink. Gray. Blink.

Everything fades so quickly as the sounds grow muted.

"Payback's a bitch," Selene screams as my vision goes blurry and then fades to black. I try to fight it, but I can't.

Wake up!

Open your eyes!

But I can't. Oh God.

The last thing I hear before everything goes silent is the sound of my daughter, *zoí mou*, crying for me. Needing me.

Needing to be saved. And I pray that Kostas is somewhere close. And that, just like in Zoe's storybooks, the monsters lose, and the dark knight saves the princesses.

But sadly, we all know too well that reality rarely imitates fiction.

chapter
fifteen

Kostas

MY MIND IS ON ONE TRACK. FIND AND KILL THE man shooting at us. The quicker I can eliminate this threat, the quicker I can find my fucking brother.

"Radio to everyone," I hiss out to Adrian, though I can't see him. "I want this place surrounded. No one leaves."

The static of his device can be heard as he makes the command. My phone buzzes in my sweats' pocket, but I can't answer just yet. Not when I'm crouched and running between vehicles hunting down a man.

Pop! Pop! Pop!

Bullets whiz past me, but I duck down just in time. It's dark and pouring down rain, so most likely he's just shooting in our general direction rather than having eyes on us. Something crunches ahead and then a man makes a grunting sound as though he fell. I charge his way. A form is rising to his feet and I don't waste any time.

Pop!

My bullet hits him in his lower stomach and he groans

from the impact. He drops his weapon to apply pressure to the wound. Adrian flies up out of nowhere and tackles the fucker.

"Get him to the cellar," I growl. I'm blinded by the rain that's running from my hair into my eyes and everything fucking hurts. I'll need to get my shit dealt with because I won't be able to run on adrenaline forever.

I stumble a little, my hip screaming in pain, but manage to keep myself upright. My phone buzzes again. "I need to check on Talia," I bark out at Adrian. "Let's get this asshole there for questioning. Aris is still missing." My blood runs cold with fear that he might have gotten to her.

Men are staked out around the villa.

Aris would have to go through an entire army of men to get to her.

She has a gun and knows how to use it.

It provides some semblance of relief, but not much. Just as we push into the groundskeeper's house, I dig my phone out of my soaked pants pocket. Adrian hauls the fucker to the cellar while I wait in the living room. My hands are shaking and it takes a few tries before I'm able to enter my code to open it.

The door flies open behind me. I'm on autopilot as I sling my AR around, ready to spray bullets into my assailant. As soon as I see who it is, I nearly fall to my knees in relief.

"Kostas!"

It takes me all of two seconds to take in her appearance. She's soaked to the bone from the rain, but so many things click into place all at once.

Blood smeared all over her teeth and running down her chin.

Blond hair matted to her face and clothes clinging to her form.

Giant bruise on the side of her face.

Sobbing. Sobbing. Sobbing.

Gun shaking hard in her grip.

No baby. No baby.

No. Fucking. Baby.

"Where's Zoe?" I demand, terror burning through me like accelerant to an already out of control inferno.

She falls against me, nearly knocking me over. I toss the AR to the couch to hug her to me.

"Talia, where the fuck is our daughter?" My chest hurts and violence thrums through me.

"T-They took her," she sobs. "You said we were s-safe. We were n-not safe."

Guilt and fury wage war inside me.

I left them alone. I thought I could eliminate the threat.

"Who?" I ask, my voice low and deceptively calm.

She looks up at me, her bottom lip wobbling. "Aris and Selene."

I should have known Aris wouldn't storm the gates so brazenly. That he'd have a plan of attack that would throw me off.

"Adrian," I bellow. "Get a car and let's go."

Three seconds later, Adrian storms into the living room. I don't have to say the words because he takes in our appearances and mutters out, "Motherfucker!" He rushes out into the night as I walk Talia out the door to wait for him to bring up a vehicle. Soon, he arrives with an SUV and I pile into the front while Talia jumps in the middle row seating behind us.

"Where to?" Adrian demands.

I scrub my palm over my face to swipe away some of

the water. The asshole hid from me for an entire year right under my nose. He's a sneaky bastard like that. But now it won't be so easy. He'll have an infant in tow and a mouthy bitch. Someone will see him. I need every goddamn person looking for him.

"Airport," I utter, though I'm not sure he'll try that. The jet is always fueled and ready. At the very least, I want to make sure he's not leaving Crete Island.

Adrian hauls ass through the dark. My fingers tremble as I dial Basil.

"Yeah, Boss?"

"Make them talk, but don't kill them. I need answers." I close my eyes and breathe heavily. "They took Zoe."

"Aris?" he growls.

"I need you to have the men eliminate the threat at the hotel. Get the bodies out of there and make sure the hotel guests are okay."

"Minister of Public Order?" he asks.

"I'll call Josef. Just clean up the fucking mess and keep the roaches on a leash in the cellar. I want to know anything, no matter how insignificant."

"Talia?"

"She's safe with us but have someone check on her mom, please."

Talia squeezes my shoulder from behind in thanks.

"On it, Boss."

After we hang up, I dial Josef. My body feels cold and I fight a tremble. Awkwardly, I fumble for the heater. Adrian shoots me a worried look before swatting my hand away to do it for me.

"This better be good," Josef growls. "I have everyone blowing up my goddamn phone."

"Terrorists after a politician," I lie. That's the lie he'll spin for me too and he'll be paid handsomely for it. "Set up a press release for the morning. They took my daughter."

He barks out some orders to someone before saying, "No shit?"

"I need…" I suck in a deep breath, blinking away a wave of dizziness. "I need you to have your men out there looking for my brother."

"Aris did this shit? Your father would be disappointed."

No, Father would have already found him and put a bullet through his skull. I'm softer than Father and it shows. I can't hold onto anything precious to me. Not my mother, not Talia for so long, not my daughter.

"Have the police looking for her. Brown hair. Blue eyes. Six months old. I'll text you a picture to send to your men."

"I'll keep it discreet. We'll find her."

I wince as I adjust my position in the seat. Blackness eats at my vision.

"And if we don't by the time of the press release tomorrow…" Josef trails off.

Adrian shakes his head at me in warning.

"Then what?" Josef asks.

"We go wide with it," I bite out. Tell all my enemies I have something I want back, even it if means presenting to them my weakness.

Josef is silent. I pull the phone away to make sure we're still connected before pressing it back to my ear.

"You heard me?" I rasp out.

"That puts a big target on your most vulnerable possession."

My heart pumps fast and furious. "Right now, I need that target to find her. Make it happen."

"Of course," he says with a sigh.

We hang up and I fade in and out the entire trip to the airport. Adrian keeps getting calls and barks out orders. My phone buzzes a few times with texts from Basil. Eventually, he sends me a text with a picture of two very freaked out looking people, but they're alive. I lift my phone to show Talia and she sobs in relief.

Melody and Stefano are okay.

My phone slips from my grip and tumbles to the floor. Talia picks it back up. Her hand is warm as it brushes along mine.

"Kostas," she cries out in alarm. "Your hand is like ice." She runs her palm along my cheek. "What's wrong with you? Are you hurt?"

"He's been hit," Adrian alerts her. "Took a bullet outside and not sure what got his arm."

"Knife," I hiss out.

Talia practically climbs onto the console to look me over. Adrian pulls up to the airport and exits the vehicle.

"You're bleeding everywhere," she whispers. "And you're so pale."

"I'll be fine," I grunt out.

"We need to get you to a hospital."

"Fuck that," I snarl. "They'll hold me when I need to be out here searching for Zoe."

Her lips press together in a worried line. "I want her just as bad as you do, but we can't look for her while you're dying on me. I need you." Tears leak from her eyes and her chin wobbles.

"But Zoe," I choke out.

"Aris never hurt her or was cruel to her," she assures me, though I hear the doubt in her voice. "He still thinks

Zoe is his. We have to have faith she's going to be okay with him."

I close my eyes, suddenly very tired. "I'm sorry I failed you."

Hysterical sobs escape her and she slaps my face, forcing my droopy eyes back open. "Don't you dare fucking take the blame for what your brother did. You have done nothing but try to protect us."

Lifting my weak arm, I swipe away her tear. "He fucking hit you."

"I hit back," she tells me icily.

"Good girl."

"I shot Selene," she whispers. "But she got away anyway."

Energy surges through me. "You put a bullet in that bitch?"

"Yes."

Gripping her neck, I pull her to me and kiss her mouth that still tastes of blood.

"You're so cold," she whimpers. "You've lost too much blood."

"I'll be okay," I assure her as I text Josef.

Me: Selene—Aris's bitch—got hit. She might need medical attention so keep eyes on the hospitals.

A wave of dizziness has my head thunking against the window. Talia slaps my face again, rousing me.

"Wake up," she says firmly. "Tell me what you need me to do."

"I need Basil to…check the footage…" I blink hard.

She grabs my phone and dials Basil. "Check the footage. See what they drove off in. Send the information to Josef."

Fuck, she listens well.

Basil says something to her and she huffs.

"If they find him, I want to see his face," she hisses. "And then I want to stab him to fucking death."

Adrian climbs back in and shakes his head. "Nothing. They didn't come here. What now?"

"We neeeed toooo," I slur, my head pounding as I try to make sense of what I'm trying to say.

"Get back to the hotel. He needs medical attention. Call his doctor because he already nixed the hospital idea. Basil's pulling up the video footage to get the make of the vehicle to send to Josef. We're going to go torture fucking answers out of the men you guys caught. And then we're going to find my baby."

"Damn," Adrian says as he peels out of the parking lot. "You've been busy."

"Oh," she sneers, "and when we find Aris, I'm going to kill him."

Adrian snorts. "You got it, Boss."

Her warm lips press to my cheek as blackness pulls me under. Hot words are whispered against my flesh that have me relaxing. "Rest, baby. I need you to get better so we can fix this. Until then, we'll take care of what we can."

I didn't marry a weak Nikolaides.

I married a goddamn mafia queen.

A Demetriou in heart and now one in soul.

chapter
sixteen

Talia

T HE DRIVE FROM THE AIRPORT BACK TO THE HOTEL is spent with me begging Kostas to stay awake. Scared if he falls asleep he might not ever wake up. His forehead is glistening with sweat, and his skin is cold and sticky to the touch. He needs a doctor sooner rather than later. I can't make out exactly where he's been shot, or how extreme it is, but based on his pale complexion, I have a feeling it's bad.

A myriad of emotions are running through me. Fear that I'm going to lose my husband and daughter. Anger that Aris would stoop this low to involve Zoe in his revenge plan. The man barely even paid attention to her the entire time we lived with him. What I told Kostas was the truth. Aris was never cruel to Zoe, but he also barely acknowledged she existed. The only reason he was keeping us there was to get back at his brother. He never even once tried to have sex with me or spend any time with Zoe, even thinking she was his daughter. Zoe and I are nothing more than tools to him. Tools to hurt his brother.

What I don't get, though, is why he didn't take me this time around… Taking me would mean hurting Kostas. And then a thought strikes me. Selene wanted me out of the picture, so the two of them could play house. Did he only take Zoe so he could keep her for him and Selene to raise? But he can barely even stand Selene. He treated her more like she was a warm body to sink his dick into when he was horny than like a potential wife.

Maybe he's hoping to use Zoe as a bargaining tool, and it was easier to take her than the both of us. Kostas did cut him out of all the business assets. Maybe he's planning to get somewhere safe and then he'll contact Kostas to make a deal. But even as I consider that, I know deep down Aris cares more about revenge than making a deal. Unless the deal involves Kostas losing everything and Aris ending up with everything.

Would Kostas give up everything he's worked his entire life creating to make sure our daughter is safe? Of course he would. But hopefully it won't come to that. I would rather find Aris and Selene and put a bullet through their cold, black hearts than hand anything of value over to them. They don't deserve anything. Not a single dollar. And definitely not the business. Hopefully whoever Kostas and his men caught will have some answers.

Kostas groans softly, his head lulling to the side, and I'm brought back to the present. Before we can do anything, we need to make sure Kostas is okay.

Adrian pulls in front of the groundskeeper's house and jumps out of the car. Basil comes running out, and between the two of them, they carry a stumbling Kostas into the house and lay him across the couch. While we wait for the doctor to arrive, I grab a knife from Basil and cut open

Kostas's shirt, needing to see how bad the damage is. As I'm assessing his body, the doctor and his assistant walk in. I've met them both when we first got home. Kostas wanted to make sure Zoe was healthy since Aris wouldn't let anyone see her. The doctor was helpful and gave her the necessary vaccines she needs.

"He has what looks like a bullet wound to his right side and a large knife gash on the back of his arm," I tell him.

He nods once and sets to work. Opening his duffle bag, he seems to have everything he needs. He begins working on Kostas's side, just above his hip, while his assistant helps him, grabbing various tools and such.

Needing to feel like I'm doing something, I grab a washcloth from a cabinet and wet it with cool water. Without getting in the way, I sit next to Kostas's head and pat his forehead with the cool washcloth.

His eyes flutter open just long enough for our eyes to meet before they close again, and my heart squeezes in my chest. I've never seen Kostas look so vulnerable and weak. He must be in so much pain.

"Did you give him pain medication?" I ask, worried he's suffering.

"Yes," the doctor responds. "But only the minimum. He doesn't like to be sedated."

His words make me realize this isn't the first time he's had to fix my husband. And that thought has me wondering how many times he's come close to dying. How many more times will his life be at risk? How long do I have with him until one day his life—or mine—is taken? I married a powerful man, who many people would love to see brought down. Every day I spend with him is on borrowed time.

The thought has me choking back a sob. If I were with

a man like Alex, this never would've happened. We'd be safe at home, running lines for an upcoming play. No, that's not true. If I were still with Alex, we would've already graduated.

But then I would've never met Kostas. I would've never known what it's like to fall in love with a man who has the ability to consume every part of my mind, body, and soul.

I would've never found myself. My sense of purpose. What I had with Alex, might've been safe, but it was boring. Alex didn't make my heart pound against my chest the way Kostas does. Going to school was fun, but it didn't pull the passion out of me like creating Pomegranate did. Alex was sweet, but he didn't challenge me the way Kostas does.

I would've never had Zoe. With her dark hair identical to her father's, and my blue eyes, she's the perfect mixture of the two of us. She's only a baby, but I can already see both of us weaved through her. My sass and determination, and Kostas's strength and bravery.

I didn't understand it at the time, but it wasn't until I married Kostas that I finally found my place in this world. It's not spitting lines in a playhouse, or traveling with friends. It's right here on this island, at this hotel with my husband and daughter. I love being Kostas's wife, being Zoe's mom.

And all I want is to be given the chance to continue to be both. Which means I need my husband to live, and I need to get my daughter back.

Right now, the only possible lead we have to go on are the men being held in the cellar. If Kostas doesn't wake up soon, I'm going to have to interrogate them myself. There's no way Kostas would want everyone sitting around waiting for him to get better while that asshole and his evil sidekick are getting farther and farther away with our daughter.

Moving the washcloth off Kostas's forehead, I lean down

to give him a kiss. "I love you," I whisper. "I need you to be okay."

Kostas groans. "You're not getting rid of me that easily." He gives me a lazy smirk that shoots straight to my belly. Butterflies. Even hurt, he can still manage to turn my insides out. He just has that effect on me.

I watch in silence while the doctor works on Kostas's side and then turns him slightly over to work on the back of his arm. After what feels like hours, the doctor sits straight and pulls off his latex gloves, handing them to his assistant.

"All done," the doctor says. "The bullet that entered his side has been removed, and he's been stitched up. An inch more to the left and it would've hit a kidney." He hands me a bottle of pills. "Here's an antibiotic for him, so it doesn't get infected."

"And the arm?" Kostas asks, shocking me when he opens his eyes and attempts to sit up.

"Whoa," I chide. "You can't move." I place my hand on his arm, and thankfully, he doesn't try to sit up anymore.

"It was deep, cut through some muscle," the doctor says. "Needed twenty stitches. But it could've been worse. Could've hit a lung." He turns his attention to Kostas. "You are very lucky. It's going to take some time for it to heal." Kostas nods in understanding. "Try to make sure not to use that arm too much while it's healing."

His assistant hands me a tiny bottle. "There's some healing cream. Apply it to both areas. The stiches will dissolve on their own in a couple of weeks."

I take my first deep breath of relief. Kostas is okay. "Thank you," I tell them both.

"Thanks, Doc," Kostas adds.

"I'll walk you out," Adrian tells them.

When Adrian returns a minute later, he reaches for Kostas, who extends his arm.

"What are you doing?" I hiss. "Lie back down!"

"Like fucking hell," Kostas says. "I've been through worse."

Stupid, stubborn fucking man!

Adrian helps my husband to his feet.

"Anything?" Kostas asks him, already back to sounding like himself. If it weren't for seeing him wince in pain, I wouldn't even know he was recently shot and stabbed.

"Nothing. None of them will speak," Adrian says. "Phoenix is still claiming he wasn't a part of it."

Phoenix? Oh my God! Phoenix was coming to visit. "You can't possibly think my brother had a part in helping Aris kidnap our daughter. She's his niece!"

"And what about Niles?" Kostas grunts. "He was brought in as well, after trying to take me out."

What the hell! "Niles is here?" I glance around, even though I know exactly where he is. "He's here, in that fucking cellar?" I shout, my blood boiling.

Kostas nods, his dark eyes flashing with violence.

"I want to see him now." I don't wait for Kostas as I stomp down to the cellar. I swing the door open and find Basil and a few of Kostas's other men standing guard. In the center of the room are three men, all tied with thick rope to their chairs. The first one I recognize as my brother. His flesh is bloody, and his head is quirked to the side, like he's slightly out of it. His eyes are closed, but I can see his chest heaving up and down. He's still alive.

The second is Niles. His face is also covered in blood, both eyes puffy and black and blue. His eyes are also closed, but he's not breathing heavy like Phoenix, so it takes me a second to determine he's still alive. For now.

The third guy I don't recognize, but he's in just as bad of shape as my brother and Niles. His eyes are open and he's glancing around him, as if trying to figure a way out. Not happening, fucker.

"Niles, wake up!" I kick his legs and his head pops up. The moment his eyes meet mine, my body trembles with anger. "You fucking asshole." I stalk closer to him and slap him across the face. "How dare you!" I cry. My hands are shaking, and my heart is beating erratically against my ribcage. How could he do this to me? To his own flesh and blood? It wasn't bad enough he used me to pay off his debt, but now he works with Aris to help steal my daughter?

"Sunshine," Niles cries out, and the nickname he used to call me has me seeing red.

"Don't you ever call me that!" I backhand him this time, and his face whips to the side. "Do you have any idea what you just did?" I grab his chin between my fingers and force him to look at me. "Do you?"

"I had to," he chokes out. "Aris has been holding me captive. It was either help him bring down Kostas or die." He thinks he chose his life over Kostas's...

"You didn't help take down Kostas," I spit. "You helped kidnap my daughter!" With no outlet for my built up aggression and frustration, I smack him across the face again. "He took my baby! And you helped him!"

Niles's eyes go wide. "Kostas's men said you had a baby, but I didn't know. I swear, Talia, I never knew anything about a baby. Aris never said a word."

I stare into his eyes for a long moment to gauge his reaction. He's telling the truth. I can see it in his eyes. The pain of knowing he helped take my daughter. It doesn't excuse what he's done, but it means he's no help. Useless.

"He doesn't know anything," I whisper, mostly to myself. Niles not knowing anything means there are only two other people in here who might know something about where Aris and Selene have taken Zoe.

I turn my attention to my brother. "Phoenix." When I say his name, he lifts his head. I don't even need to ask him. I know my brother. He loves me and would never do anything to help Aris in taking my daughter. I heard his voice over the phone. He was excited to be an uncle.

"You know damn well I wasn't a part of this," Phoenix growls, his voice strong and deadly.

"And why the fuck should we believe you?" I turn around to find Kostas standing behind me. "It won't be the first time you've followed in your daddy's footsteps," Kostas sneers. I'm not sure how long he's been here—I was too focused on Niles—but his color is almost fully back, and he's wearing a new shirt.

"I would never do that shit to my sister," Phoenix hisses.

"Kostas, I don't think he would do this," I tell my husband, needing him to believe me. Otherwise he's going to kill my brother. Phoenix might have spent his entire life working for Niles and the business, but he would never purposely put my life or my daughter's at risk. I believe that with my entire being.

"I didn't do it," Phoenix says again.

"Then prove it," Kostas says, his eyes locked on Phoenix as he slowly walks over to him. Once he's standing in front of him, he glances at Basil. "Hand me your knife."

Adrian steps forward. "Boss…" I know what he's silently not saying. *Let me handle this.* Kostas is too weak to torture anyone. But if Adrian says it out loud it will make

Kostas appear weak. And Kostas would rather die than ever appear weak in front of his men, or especially, his enemies.

"I got it," Kostas hisses. He snatches the knife out of Basil's hand and slices the rope holding Phoenix down. Then he slices the rope holding his hands together. "You say you didn't have a part in helping my brother kidnap my daughter… Okay. But your fucking father did. Caught him red-handed with a fucking gun, shooting at me. You have a choice to make."

Phoenix clenches his jaw, and his furious gaze flits from Kostas, to me, and then to Niles, who is now wide awake and staring at his son.

Phoenix stands and stalks over to Kostas, until their chests are practically touching. "I don't have to prove shit to you," Phoenix says.

I hold my breath in fear of what's to come. If Phoenix doesn't do something, Kostas will kill him without hesitating.

Phoenix's hateful glare leaves Kostas, and he turns toward Niles. "You did this shit to yourself," he says in a lowly, distant voice.

"Son, please," Niles begs. "I didn't have a choice. You have to believe me."

"Shut your fucking mouth!" Phoenix roars. "You chose yourself over your fucking daughter for the last time." My brother stalks toward the guard standing closest to Niles, grabs the gun from his holster, and aims it at Niles's chest.

"This is for everything you've done to Talia."

Pop!

Crimson bleeds through Niles's shirt as he cries out in shock. He hit him in the stomach, not the heart—keeping him alive. Before he can beg Phoenix not to kill him, Phoenix aims the gun at his forehead.

135

Instinctively, I slam my eyes closed, already knowing what's coming.

"And this is for Zoe."

Pop!

I open my eyes back up. Nile's head has been blown to bits. Several of the guards have blood splattered on them. My stomach roils at the sight, but I force the bile down, refusing to look weak in front of all these men. He got what he deserved.

My gaze goes to the third man. He's staring at Niles, his eyes wide-open in shock and fear.

"What do you know about Aris taking my daughter?" I ask him.

"I don't know anything!" he exclaims. "I was just told to come here and kill as many men as possible."

"He doesn't know shit," Kostas growls. "Nobody fucking does because Aris was too smart to let anybody know."

Kostas pulls the gun out from behind him and shoots the guy dead in the heart. His life ends so quickly, his eyes remain open as if he's frozen in place.

My eyes flit back and forth between the two dead men as reality hits. "Kostas," I cry. He turns his attention to me. "If nobody knows anything, how are we going to get our little girl back?"

Kostas walks over to me, and as tightly as his broken body can, he wraps me in his arms as I sob into his chest. We have no more leads. There are no breadcrumbs to follow. Nobody knows anything. It's as if Aris and Selene have vanished with Zoe. "Shh," Kostas coos, his body shaking from the pain he must be in. "We're going to find her. I promise."

chapter
seventeen

Kostas

I STARE AT MY REFLECTION AS I BRUSH MY TEETH. COLD. Furious. A monster. Certainly not one who looks like the father of a small, perfect baby. Or the lover and husband of a beautiful woman. I'm ruthless. My father's son. Every bit the Demetriou I need to be to face the media.

Because *they* will see.

My enemies.

And I need them to see who the fuck they're dealing with.

Talia enters the bathroom as I angrily scrub the film off my teeth. I barely slept two hours, but the press will be here at eight sharp this morning, and if I have any hope for making it through today, I need coffee and a motherfucking bagel.

"I've never heard anyone growl while brushing their teeth before," she says, her eyes squinting and her voice gravelly from sleep.

I spit, then rinse, before drying my mouth off. I've already showered for the day, which was agony on my wounds, and am in just a towel. My wife looks stunning somehow in one of my oversized T-shirts. Her blond hair is in disarray. But what has me seeing red is the awful bruising and split lip. The entire side of her face is dark purple and blue.

He touched what's mine.

He *has* what's mine.

Aris always thought he could battle with me, and because he was fucking blood, I played his games. Enjoyed taunting him whenever I could. In a way, it was our screwed-up way of bonding. But then he crossed the line. Raped my goddamn woman. Stole her and kept her from me. And now he took my child.

Loyalty means nothing to that Demetriou.

Loyalty means everything to me.

This means fucking war.

When Talia was gone, I drifted. Lost in a fog of confusion and anger. Aris played me. Dangled me by his strings and reveled in my torment. Talia made me soft. I *wanted* to be soft for her. Only for her. But clearly, I softened in a way that exposed my weakness. I may as well have given Aris a fucking gun and said, "Point and shoot here."

For the last year, he's had a "blind me" on his side. He had money and resources. He had my lack of knowledge.

But now he's no longer battling a brother, he's in a war with a monster. He thought he could sneak into my compound and get away with this shit. Sadly, he was mistaken. I will gut Greece. Burn it to the motherfucking ground. I will fill every hole with gasoline and light it on fire. Every roach will come out of hiding and I will smash them until I find the rat.

Aris will be mine.

And I'll get my daughter back.

"Kostas," Talia says, her brows furrowing. "Are you okay?"

I gently grip her jaw and tilt her head to the side so I can inspect every dark shade of the abuse she endured yesterday. With the barest of a kiss, I whisper it over her sore flesh. My words of hate are breathed against her skin.

"He will pay for this."

She shivers and grips my wrist. I turn slightly to find her lips. Despite the cut on her lip, I kiss her hard enough to split it back open. The sweet, metallic taste of her mixes with the minty toothpaste, making me hunger for her more than any bagel this morning. If I had more time, I'd turn my aggressions into passion so I could whisper all my evil promises against her skin—promises to take out our enemy and bring home our treasure.

My phone buzzes and I nip at her sore lip once before I pull away.

Adrian: Press is already lined up at the gate. Josef is waiting, too. Where are we doing this?

Me: Hotel lobby. Send Josef to my office. I want to meet with him before we go public.

Adrian: On it.

"I have to meet with the Minister of Public Order. Then, I'll be doing a press release." I stroke my fingers through her hair that hangs in messy, natural-dry waves after the shower she took alone last night while I crashed into bed. "I need you to look the part of an angel."

Not that she'll have any trouble doing so.

Her brows furrow. "Why? What's going on?"

My perfect Talia and her never-ending quest for answers.

I drop my towel and nod at her to follow me while I dress. Throwing on some boxers and socks, I then make my way into our closet. The mess had been cleaned up by hotel staff before we went to bed, but the feeling of failure washes over me.

Zoe was taken from this very closet.

Talia lingers in the doorway, no doubt feeling sadness over last night and what went down in here. As I dress in a suit, she runs her fingers over one of her white dresses. She pulls it off the hanger and holds it up.

"This one?"

I rake my gaze down the serene, silky white material. "Perfect. And don't you dare cover up what he did to you. They need to see."

Her blue eyes dart back and forth. "Who? Who will need to see?"

Snagging a blue tie that matches her eyes, I slide it around my neck and begin knotting it. Once I've tightened it at my throat, I let out a heavy sigh of resignation.

"You are married to the monster Greece knows. Well, at least the one all the scum knows. *I* will reach them. I'm a Demetriou, it's what we do. But you," I say with a smile as I grab my jacket off a hanger. "*You* will reach the regular people. Every man, woman, and child in all of Europe. We're going to hit them from all sides. Just be you and you'll do exactly what I need you to." I step into my shoes and then walk over to her. "And you're going to have to let me be me."

"What exactly does that mean?"

"It means, I'm soft with you. In here, with our family, soft is good." My features morph into something wicked and furious. "But out there, I need to be a blade forged in stone. I need to be unbreakable. I need to be powerful." I start to put my jacket on, but my arm winces in pain.

She purses her lips before dropping the dress in favor

of helping me. She takes the jacket and holds it open so I can gingerly slide my bad arm into the sleeve. Once I have it pulled on and buttoned, I turn to regard her.

"You're hurting," she breathes. "Physically and in here." Her palm presses to my chest between my pectorals. "It's okay to be vulnerable. Our daughter is gone. They hurt us."

Sweet, innocent, pure angel.

I slide my fingers beneath her chin and tilt her head up. Blue eyes sparkle at me. She's so fucking strong. Only a woman like Talia could ever have the backbone and fire to be able to stand beside a Demetriou. She's fearless and determined. A fucking storm.

"Out there, I can't be. It's the only way to get Zoe back. The public needs an angel and the Underworld needs a fiery, unstoppable king." I kiss her nose. "Are we in this together?"

She smiles. "Since the day I saw you in that courtyard."

"You tried to run," I say, in a slightly playful tone.

"I wanted you to catch me."

Reluctantly, I pull away, needing to get a move on the day. "Make sure you grab something to eat. Basil will escort you. There'll be coffee and bagels in the lobby if you want that."

"I was thinking fruit. A pomegranate sounds good."

She pulls off her T-shirt, revealing her round tits and rosy nipples. Fuck, she does my head in when all I need is to focus.

"A pomegranate?" I ask, my voice husky as my dick strains in my slacks.

She bends to pick up the dress from the floor and holds it to her chest. Her blond hair cascades over one shoulder as she tilts her head to the side. "An angel can live in hell."

"Not without getting burned."

Sauntering over to me, she stands on her toes and kisses the corner of my mouth. "The devil wouldn't allow that."

"He already has," I growl, my palm finding her hip and squeezing possessively.

"But he won't let it happen again."

So confident and sure.

She's right.

"Go be the badass we need right now," she says, pushing on my chest to break us apart. "I'll be at my restaurant sucking on seeds until you let me suck on you later."

"Are you trying to kill me?"

"You'll need to relieve some tension and then you'll need a nap." She shrugs. "Because then we're going to go get our girl."

"Damn right."

I let my stare linger on the swell of her breasts and then up her slender throat before I latch my eyes to her parted lips. Fuck, how I want to yank her to me, drag her to the floor, and drive into her wildly. The desire to claim and own is fierce, but we have more pressing matters to attend to. And once we have our daughter back, I'll demand my fucked up happily ever after, one orgasm at a time.

Adrian flanks my right and Josef is on my left as we walk into the hotel lobby as a united front—the mob and the police coming together for the same agenda: take down Aris and find a baby. Talia will enter soon with Basil. I need to say what I need to say without her weakening my resolve. As soon as the press sees us, flashes start going off like rapid gunfire. The lights blind me, but I ignore them as I make my way to the podium that's been set up. Josef steps to the microphone first.

"Dear citizens of Crete Island," he starts, holding up his hand to end the buzzing chattering of questions being barked our way. "We're not here to answer questions, but to instead deliver a series of statements."

More flashes snap.

"Last year, good men and women of Cretan General Hospital were gunned down in a tragic terrorist event. The Demetriou family, while dealing with their own familial tragedies, were instrumental in eliminating the threat at that time." Josef gives me a grim smile to which I nod so he'll continue. "His father, the late Ezio Demetriou, was a friend to me and a pillar in this community. The philanthropic donations of this family have been what's kept the island profitable and successful. With…" He flashes me another look and I nod. "With Ezio's recent, natural passing—something the family had wished to keep quiet so they could grieve in private but are no longer able to—we are faced with terrorism once again. There are those who see the Demetrious' efforts as something to destroy, making these attempts when they are down. Last night, they tried to do exactly that. But they are wrong. Our people and the Demetrious aren't broken so easily. We will fight for peace and profit."

He steps away from the podium and gestures for me to take his place. I keep my features cool and impassive. Whenever I lock stares with a reporter, they cower under my gaze and look away.

"My family is the proud owner of the Pérasma Hotel. Last night, men stormed our gates and tried to destroy what we built." *Men ordered by my brother.* "Because we take security extremely seriously, none of our guests were hurt or even saw the terrible situation unfold. We lost a few good men protecting the people at our hotel."

More flashes go off as reporters demand to know the names.

I raise my hand, effectively silencing them all. "They were hired on to do a job for the Demetriou family. And they did it well. But now we need for you all to do your job."

A flash of white in the back of the room indicates Talia has arrived. She's clutching a soft pink blanket and a newly framed picture of Zoe. Basil escorts my wife past the curious onlookers and to the podium with me. I pull her close, sharing the microphone with her.

"I'm a private man," I say, my voice hard as steel. "I keep my personal life out of the spotlight. Because of my influence in Greece, people think they can use my personal life as a weakness against me." I lean over to inhale Talia's sweet scent before kissing the top of her head, earning more pops of flashes. I turn back to the crowd, my glare once again affixed. "Last year, I wed the woman I loved in a secret ceremony for just the two of us. But then she was taken from me." People demand to know by whom, but I ignore them. Everyone underground knows it was Aris and that's all that matters. "When I found her again, she brought home a Demetriou princess. My strong, resilient wife survived the atrocities of capture, delivered our daughter while in captivity, and found the strength to make her way back to me."

Talia starts to cry and clings to me, which sends the media into a frenzy.

"Last night, while we worked to keep our people safe, the terrorists came in and took our daughter."

144

The press starts shouting, horrified and demanding answers.

"She's…" I trail off and swallow hard. "My wife, Talia, would like to speak about her."

She sniffles as she pulls away slightly. "Our little girl Zoe was kidnapped." Her body trembles as she holds the blanket to her and shows the crowd the picture. "She's sweet and curious and laughs and…" A sob chokes her. "Oh God, I just want her back in my arms."

I stroke my fingers through her hair in a possessive way while staring down every camera in the room, commanding them with one look. *Find my fucking daughter and bring her to me alive.*

"I beg of you," Talia pleads. "If anyone knows anything, please help us. We need her. She doesn't deserve this."

"Our fine Minister of Public Order has set up a call center to take any and all calls. Calls leading to the finding of our daughter will be handsomely rewarded," I say into the microphone. This is for the normal, everyday citizens. They'll look for her because that's what good people do, money or not. They want to reunite a child with their family.

But I need the bad people looking too.

"Fifty million dollars."

The room explodes with excitement.

"She was last seen with Aris Demetriou and Selene Vincent." The crowd gasps again. I ramble through their physical descriptions while deliberately leaving off the fact Aris is my brother. They all know this. I don't need to fucking say it. Everyone underground will see this as one concrete fact: Aris Demetriou is dead to me.

"Twenty-four hours. If she's found within that time frame, I'll reward the finder additionally in ways I see fit."

Meaning, they will get a favor with the Demetrious, which is priceless. "Thank you all for your help."

The group goes wild with questions, and seven of my men have to flank us to get us away from the crowd. Once we're safely inside my office, I give Adrian a nod to clear the lobby of the press and tell him to apprise me of any new developments. The moment I have the door closed and locked, I collect my emotional wife in my arms.

"You did great," I murmur against her hair. "We need everyone's help in finding her."

"I miss her," she whimpers.

"Me too, *moró mou.*"

She tilts her head up to look at me, her eyes red and swollen from her crying. "The people who hate you know everything now. That your father's dead. That you're married. That you have Zoe. That your brother betrayed you. You showed your hand, Kostas."

I sweep my palm delicately over her bruised cheek and then run my fingers through her hair. "It was the only way to get her back. We *will* get her back."

"What if someone hurts her to get back at you?" she whispers, a fat tear rolling down her cheek.

I kiss the wetness on her skin and close my eyes. "We have to trust that money talks. The only one who cares about revenge over money is Aris. The citizens of Crete Island and every piece of scum who knows the Demetriou name will be hunting for our little girl. There's no way we can know where Aris went and turning over every stone would take precious time we don't have. All we can do is let the people do what we can't. We have to trust this will work."

"What if it doesn't work?"

"It's our only option, Talia."

"I'm scared."

"I know," I breathe against her soft lips. "I'm doing the best I can."

"I know you are and I love you for that."

Her lips press forcefully to mine as a fierce growl leaves her throat. The kiss takes me by surprise, especially when her hands begin frantically sliding my jacket off my shoulders and sending it to the floor before yanking at my belt. My cock—ever ready to play with his favorite pussy—stiffens in my slacks. Pre-cum leaks from me as the desperate need to fill her overtakes me. She pulls my dick from its confines and kneels before me.

"Talia," I rumble, my fist grabbing into her hair, ready to pull her back up to my level. I pause to admire how fucking gorgeous she is.

Her blue eyes are intent and dark with lust as her tongue slides between her plump lips and flicks against my wet tip. A hiss rushes past my teeth as I stare at the angel queen who bows before her evil king. Pure wickedness gleams in her eyes as she circles my slit with her hot tongue, her expression equal parts hungry and taunting. I could pull her up to her feet and fuck her senseless, but I'm mesmerized by her devious stare and pretty mouth that's stained the color of pomegranate from breakfast. She slides her mouth over the crown and a growl rumbles from me. I close my eyes, dizzied by the bliss. Her mouth bobs up and down over my length as she desperately feeds my cock into her hungry mouth. When her teeth scrape my tender flesh as she tries to take me deep in her throat, the need to have her completely overwhelms me.

"Stand up," I command. "I need to be inside you."

Her mouth pops off my dick as she shakily rises to her

feet. I waste no time grabbing her full ass and lifting her. She fuses her swollen lips to mine and kisses me just as she was my dick a moment ago. I shove her against the wall as I reach between us to grip my cock. She moans when I slide my tip along her wet slit over her panties, seeking the tight warmth only her body can gift to me. I push the head of my dick under the side hem of her panties to tease her bare flesh with my own and seek entrance. With a painful flex of my hips, I drive all the way into her, her wet panties rubbing along the side of my dick as lubricant. As I fuck my wife against the wall, I can feel the burn as my stitches tear free. I could opt for a better position, but only one goal is in my mind.

Take Talia.

I grip her ass with one hand and squeeze her tit with the other as I drive into her hard. Her mouth owns mine as she fucks my mouth with her tongue. Her thighs tighten around my waist, only further irritating my wound. I'm about to come, but a wave of dizziness has me struggling to keep Talia upright. With her still on my dick, I carry her over to my desk. I sit her ass down on the surface and then push her back, breaking our kiss. She whimpers at the loss.

"Pull your dress up your hips and let me see what I'm fucking," I rasp out, ignoring the pain lancing through my body.

She yanks up the material, fisting it just under her breasts that jiggle each time I drive into her. Her heels rest on the edge of the desk and her thighs are parted open in a dirty, inviting way that makes me want to recreate this moment later when our life is back to normal and I can call her filthy names like my "needy little slut." Names I know will turn her on while getting nasty in my office, but names that don't quite fit the moment.

"Touch me," she commands, her blue eyes intense as she drags me away from the fact that our daughter is still missing and nothing will be normal until she's found. "Right now, it's just us, Kostas."

Failure and loss fade for the moment as I run my fingers along her throbbing clit over her panties. She cries out in surprise when I rip the fabric apart and toss it away. Her hips lift and she clenches around my cock. I easily circle my fingers in a way that strums my wife into having the most beautiful sounds leave her lips.

Someone knocks on the door and we both grind out words at the same time.

"Go the fuck away!"

"We'll be out in a minute!"

Our eyes lock and I thrust hard against her, pinching her clit in tandem with each glide inside her. When I notice blood on her leg, I run my free fingers through it, marveling at the smears along her tanned flesh. Her body seizes with pleasure and her breasts jut forward as her back arches. I'm captivated with how wild and so damn beautiful she is as her pussy squeezes the fuck out of me. I groan, nearly collapsing as my balls tighten and then my release spurts furiously inside her. Cum leaks out as I slide in and out of her, filling her with everything I have. When I'm wrung dry, I slip from her hot body and stagger back, trembling and my still-hard dick dripping.

"Fucking gorgeous," I hiss, my eyes raking down her perfect body and settling at her pussy.

Bright red and raw from being fucked hard.

Thick, white cum runs down her used slit toward her ass crack.

Shaking thighs as she recovers from her orgasm.

I step closer despite the spinning around me and collect my cum on my finger. Our eyes meet when I push it back into her needy body. She whimpers and squirms as I fuck my jizz back into her cunt with just my finger. Once I'm sure it's deep inside where it belongs, I curl my finger up and seek out the part of her that'll make her scream. She shakes her head as though she can't take any more, which only urges me to show her she can. I add another finger and press the hot, throbbing spot inside her until she grips the edge of the desk with both hands and bellows my name. Her hips ride up, doing their own little dance to meet the movement of my fingers until she comes down from her high. I slip my hand away from her and admire the dark, pink depths that remain open and inviting to me. With one clench, she hides that part of herself from me, sending more cum pushing out of her pussy.

"I need…" she whispers, closing her thighs. "I need to shower and change and eat and…oh my God, you're bleeding!"

I shrug as I glance down at my white dress shirt that's seeping with blood. "It was worth it."

She sits up and then stands in front of me. Her dress falls into place and I want to pout over the fact that I can't watch my cum slide down her inner thighs. "Let's go home and get cleaned up so we can find our girl."

"Talia," I growl as I grip her throat and draw her to me. I press my lips to hers. "I love you."

Her lips break into a smile—one that's been missing the past twelve hours. "I love you too."

"We're going to find her."

"I know we are."

chapter
eighteen

Talia

I T'S BEEN FIVE DAYS SINCE KOSTAS AND I STOOD IN front of all of Greece and pleaded with the people to help locate our little girl. Five days since he offered them millions of dollars to locate Aris and Selene. And it's been five long as hell days of sifting through the thousands of leads that end in nothing but dead ends. Everybody wants a chance at the money, which means everybody thinks they've seen our little girl. I've sat in Kostas's office with him and his men for hours upon hours, clicking on lead after lead, blowing up image after image, hoping to spot one of them. I've seen several dozen redheaded women, hundreds of men in suits, and I've looked at enough babies that they all have blurred into one of the same. But none of them are the people we're looking for.

It wasn't until my eyes were itchy and I felt like I was going cross-eyed that Kostas ganged up on me with my mom and made me go home to take a break. I begged and pleaded, but they insisted.

"*Cara mia*," Mom coos. "Please, you have to eat

something." She pushes the homemade chicken soup closer to me. The aroma fills my nostrils and my stomach growls in hunger. I can't even remember the last time I ate something besides an energy bar. "You need to be strong for your little girl, and in order to be strong, you must take care of yourself."

She leans in and rubs her thumbs along my cheeks and then under my eyes. "You have dark circles under your eyes. You need to sleep."

"I have slept," I argue, pulling my face out of her grasp.

"More than a couple hours," Phoenix adds. He's been staying at the hotel, helping to check out any leads that come through that Kostas feels are worth investigating further, which is almost all of them. My husband is determined to find our daughter, and if there's a slight possibility someone's lead could be the one that takes us to her, he wants it investigated. He has hundreds of men scouring the country on top of the thousands of leads that are being emailed and called in.

And with each passing hour, each lead that hits a wall, I get more anxious that Aris has disappeared where nobody can find them.

"Talia, please," Mom begs. "Just a few bites."

Not wanting to argue with them, I bring the spoon to my lips. But before I can take a bite, I imagine my daughter locked up somewhere with Aris and Selene, hungry and tired and cold, and a sob racks through my entire body. I drop the spoon back into the bowl, and hot liquid splashes out, burning my hand. "How am I supposed to eat when I don't even know if my little girl is being fed?" I push the bowl away. There's no way I can eat until I know she's safe in my arms and her tummy is full.

I stand at the same time Mom does. She envelops me in her arms and I breathe in her floral scent. "What if she's hungry?" I cry out. "Or lonely?" My entire body shakes against my mom's as she holds me tight. I can feel an anxiety attack coming on, but I already know I won't be able to stop it. I've been having them every day since Zoe was taken. "What if they've hurt her…or worse…" I can't even finish my sentence. My words are cut off with my cries. My head pounds so hard it feels like my entire body is vibrating. My heart is racing, and my legs feel like noodles.

"Talia, you have to calm down," she says as I begin to hyperventilate. She walks us over to the couch and helps me to sit. I try to take in gulps of air, but it's hard to breathe. My sweet little baby is somewhere out there with two crazy psychos who don't love her. They don't even care about her. Anything can happen to her, and every second she's gone is less of a chance of ever finding her alive.

Stefano appears in front of me with a glass of water. "Here, sweetheart, take these." He extends his hand with two pills, but I shake my head.

"No, I need to be awake and lucid in case a solid lead comes in." The last thing I want is to be out cold when my daughter needs me.

"Talia, you can't keep going like this," Mom demands. "Please, it will help you to calm down and rest. If a lead comes through, we'll wake you up. Kostas is handling it."

I want to argue with them, but they're right. I haven't slept in what feels like days. My body is over exhausted and shaking like a leaf in a storm.

With trembling hands, I take the glass and pills from Stefano. After swallowing them, my mom pulls me back into her side and rocks me until my body gives up and my eyes close.

My eyes flutter open, and when I look around, I see I'm in my bed. I listen for Zoe. The villa is quiet. Is she sleeping? What time is it? Does Kostas have her? And then I remember she's not here. She's missing. And my heart cracks all over again.

My phone vibrates on the end table and I grab it to see who is calling. Kostas. I check the time. It's ten o'clock at night. I've been sleeping for almost eight hours thanks to the pills Stefano gave me.

I quickly answer the call, hoping he has good news. "Have you found her?"

"No, there's been no leads that have panned out."

My heart falls into my stomach. No leads. In a couple hours, it's going to hit midnight and it will be another day without my baby girl.

"I was calling to check on you," he adds. His voice sounds worried. My mom must've told him I had another anxiety attack.

"Are you in your office?" I ask, sitting up and throwing the blankets off me.

"I am, but you need to get some sleep," Kostas says softly.

"I've been sleeping all afternoon. I'll be there in a few minutes."

I shower quickly, get dressed, and brush my teeth to get rid of the bad taste in my mouth. Then, I head to Kostas's office, Basil hot on my trail. I'm thankful for my ever-present shadow. Mom and Stefano must've gone back to their villa for the night.

On the way, I see Phoenix walking down the pathway. He gives me a sad smile. "I was checking out another lead," he says. "Another dead end."

"Thank you for helping." I wrap my arms around his waist and give him a hug.

"There's nowhere else I would be," Phoenix assures me. "We're going to find her, Talia."

I want to believe him, but with each passing day, my hopes are shattered more and more. None of it makes any sense. If Aris wanted money, he would've contacted us by now. If he wanted to use her as a bargaining chip to steal the business from Kostas, he would've reached out. And since Kostas made sure to announce publicly that Ezio is dead, Aris has to know by now that his father is no longer alive.

But he's been completely silent. And that's what worries me. If he took her with the intent to keep her, he could be anywhere by now, and we may never see her again. At least if he took her with the purpose of using her to negotiate, we could give him what he wants and get our daughter back. The problem is Aris believes Zoe is his. A lie I told at the time to save us, but now regret.

As I walk through the doors of the office, I see Kostas and a thought hits me. "Kostas." He glances my way and walks toward me. "You told the world that Zoe is your daughter."

"Yeah…" Kostas gives me a confused look.

"Aris thought she was his. If he heard your speech, he knows she's not his." My hands cover my mouth as I remember what Aris said to me when I told him Zoe was his.

"Talia, talk to me," Kostas demands.

"Aris warned me that if he ever found out the baby wasn't really his, I would pay." I lied to him for over a year, swore up and down the baby was his… "What if he took her to use her as a bargaining chip, but once he found out she wasn't really his, he changed his mind?" My heart begins to race, and my head feels cloudy. Another anxiety attack is surfacing. "He could be keeping her just to make me pay." This could be all my fault. I never should've lied to Aris.

"Talia, calm down," Kostas says, taking me in his arms. "It doesn't matter what Aris knows or doesn't know. It changes nothing. You told him what he needed to hear to keep you and our little girl safe. We're going to find her."

"Boss," Adrian calls Kostas over. "Check out this image." He blows up a picture on the computer screen. It's of a man who meets Aris's description carrying a baby, but we can't see any faces.

"Where was this taken?" Kostas asks.

"The airport about thirty minutes ago," Adrian says.

"He wouldn't just walk through the airport," I say out loud. Aris is too smart for that, even if the man holding the baby looks almost identical to him.

"Probably not," Kostas agrees. "But we're following every possible lead."

He looks over his shoulder. "Phoenix," he barks. "Airport." Without asking any questions, Phoenix comes over and gets the information from Adrian then takes off.

We spend the next couple hours going through emails and calls of leads. When it's nearly four in the morning and I can tell Kostas is dragging, I tell him we need to go home. He looks like he wants to argue, but doesn't.

When we get home, he takes a quick shower and meets me in bed. With his arms around me, I snuggle into the crook of his neck. "Six days," I whisper. Tomorrow it will be a week.

"We're going to find her," Kostas says for a millionth

time, his voice filled with as much conviction as the first time he said it.

As my eyes are closing, his phone rings loudly throughout the room. He leans over and answers it. "Yeah." He sits up straight, knocking my head off his body. "You sure?" I can't hear who he's speaking to, but whoever it is, is talking fast. "I'll check right now."

Kostas places the phone on speaker and pulls up his email app. Peering over, I look to see what was emailed, and right there in color is a picture of Selene holding our daughter.

"That's her!" I gasp.

chapter
nineteen

Kostas

"ON MY WAY," I GROWL, SLINGING MY BODY OUT of the bed on a frantic hunt for clothes. "Pick me up in front of my villa in two minutes."

Talia flies out of the bed and starts dressing. "I can't believe they found her. Is it close? How long until we get there—"

"Not we," I bark out as I button my jeans and yank on a white T-shirt. "Me."

"Hell no," she screeches as she throws on her own clothes. "I'm going."

I don't have time to fight with her on this. All I do have time for is to grab my Glock from the bedside drawer and stalk out of the bedroom. Talia comes trotting after me. When I open the door, Basil is standing beside Adrian's SUV, talking to him.

"Hold down the fort," I bark out to Basil.

He nods before stepping away. I open the rear door and assist Talia in getting in before climbing into the front passenger seat.

Talia starts to sob in the back seat. When I glance back, I see that Adrian already loaded up the car seat. He feels it too. We're bringing her home. Thank fuck we have the cover of the dark, early morning. The last thing I need is for someone to tip Aris off.

Adrian hauls ass out of the hotel property and gets onto the main road. When he'd emailed me the pictures, he also emailed the location. Two hours from here on the other side of Crete Island near a small airport. Aris may have thought about trying to leave via plane but decided against it at the last minute because he has to know I have eyes everywhere, especially ports and airports. The motel we're headed to is a piece of shit one that hookers and johns use. I cringe thinking what sort of cesspool my baby's living in right now.

"Who'd the tip come from?" I ask as we drive.

"A maid."

"Just a maid?"

"Just a maid."

"Good," I grunt. "We won't owe any roaches shit. You'll have to get the maid to safety. The moment we wire her the money, she'll have a target on her back."

"Zoe first, maids later," Talia offers from the back seat.

I look over my shoulder and smile. "Zoe is always first."

The two-hour drive is tense and quiet. I answer calls and check in on different people. My main concern is Aris and Selene getting tipped off before we arrive. Soon, we're creeping through a small town twenty minutes from the coast. The sun has risen and a few restaurants blink their signs offering hot breakfast, making my stomach growl.

Zoe first, coffee and bagels later.

"It's up here," Adrian says.

"I'll go around front and you check the back," I order to him.

"I'm going with you," Talia says, trying her shit with me again.

I whip around and reach for her hand, pulling her close to me. With my eyes burning into hers, I kiss the back of her hand. "Not today."

"But—"

"I need you safe inside the SUV ready to drive off. Understood, *moró mou*? If Adrian and I should get injured, I need to be able to pass Zoe off to you and you get the fuck out of here. Please, for once in your stubborn fucking life listen to me." My words are spoken harshly to her, but I can't keep my wits about me if she's behind me. No fucking way. I need to be able to act without question.

Fat tears well in Talia's blue eyes, but she nods, sending them loose from her lids and skating down her cheeks.

"I love you," I whisper to her. "I *need* you to do this."

"I *can* do this," she says fiercely, swiping at her tears with her free hand. "I love you too."

I kiss her hand once more before releasing her to pull my Glock out of the center console and readying myself to act. Adrian parks a little ways up the road where we can see the small, aging, and decrepit motel, pointed toward the main road for a fast getaway. Several cars litter the parking lot.

"Which unit?" I demand.

"The maid said room six there on the end of the east side."

"We'll walk over to the west side and split around the building from there. Shoot first, ask questions later. At this point, put a bullet in Aris's skull. We can't risk him getting away. Zoe's safety is our primary concern." As much as I want to torture the fuck out of him, I can't let it cloud my judgment.

Adrian and I climb out of the SUV. When I glance back, I can see Talia scrambling to the front seat. Good girl. With my Glock ready, I nod at Adrian and then quietly walk along the front of the motel. He disappears around back. I pass by rooms one through three without incident, but when I get to the fourth room, I hear muffled crying not far off.

Zoe.

Panic swells up inside me and I quicken my pace, no longer worried about hiding. My sole focus is my daughter, whose crying gets louder the closer to room six I get. When I make it to the door, I press my ear to it.

"Shut up, stupid baby! Just shut the fuck up!"

When I hear what sounds like a slap, I step back and kick the door in. It slams against the wall and I charge inside, my gun drawn. Selene has Zoe in her arms and picks up a gun beside her. Zoe is red-faced and squirming, clearly pissed at being struck by this psycho cunt.

"Give me my fucking baby," I bellow, my gun aimed at Selene's face.

She presses the gun against Zoe's side. "Get the hell out of here!"

I don't move. Quickly I take stock of the situation. It smells like dirty diapers and hard liquor. Beside Selene on the end table are several empty bottles of alcohol. Between those are a few of Zoe's used bottles. My daughter wears a diaper and it's full of piss, hanging off her little body. A red handprint on her little thigh makes me want to bash Selene's head into the corner of the nightstand.

"Put Zoe down and I'll let you live."

"Liar," she snarls. "That's why I'm keeping this baby."

When she digs the barrel of the gun into Zoe's side, she screams bloody murder.

Fuck.

I could put a bullet in her head, but she's holding Zoe too close to her. With the way Zoe flails and squirms, I could accidentally hit her. I can't take that chance.

"Money? You want money?" I ask, my gun still trained on her. "I'll give you money and ship your ass to another country. You don't fucking deserve it, but that'll be my trade. It's the best goddamn offer you have."

Her eyes dart to the window, her brows furrowing. "I need this baby. I need him."

She looks like shit. Her red hair is dull and stringy and she's not wearing makeup. A big blackish purple bruise mars her throat. Someone grabbed her neck hard enough to leave a mark. If I had my guess, it's that my brother's been hitting the bottle and lost his temper on her. I just hope they didn't hurt Zoe. The red mark on her leg is infuriating enough. I can't imagine more.

Zoe's screams get louder and louder. She's pissed. I'd like to think it's because she hears my voice and wants me, but she's only six months old, so that's probably not right. I don't know much about babies. What I do know is she'll be one happy kid the moment she's in her mother's arms rather than this cunt's.

"He doesn't want you," I grind out. Delusional bitch. "You were always a cover for him." That much I realize now. Had I thought he was remotely interested in Talia, I would've shaken him down a lot sooner. But the fact he pretended to love Selene and I thought he wanted to marry her, he was able to fool me.

"He does want me!" she cries out. "He loves me and one

day I'll give him a baby of our own. We won't need that stupid bitch's baby anymore!"

This is taking too long.

Adrian is probably outside wondering what's going on but won't enter, especially if he overhears me trying to talk her down. But Talia? She's probably panicking. I know her. The last thing I need is her flying in here like a loose cannon upsetting the situation even further.

"Put the gun down," I command, my voice loud and sharp.

Crash!

The motel shakes as something explodes nearby. It's enough to distract Selene to jerk her head toward the sound, dropping her guard.

Pop!

I put a bullet on the part of her body farthest from my daughter. Her foot. She screams, dropping Zoe, who rolls to the floor with a loud thud. My daughter screams—which is music to my fucking ears considering the drop to the floor—and I stalk forward. She's okay. Selene raises the gun and I put a bullet into her shoulder. Another one pierces her throat. I want to make her hurt. She gurgles, grabbing her throat as blood sprays. With my eyes on her, I scoop up Zoe, tucking her under my arm like a football. Selene gapes at me as she tries and fails to stop the blood flow.

Pop!

I hit her in the stomach. I want her to bleed to death, thinking about what she did. How she struck my goddamn daughter. How she hurt my wife. How she aided my brother in an unimaginable crime.

Tucking my gun into the back of my jeans, I pull Zoe to my chest and kiss her sweaty head. "Shh, I've got you."

Selene has slumped against the headboard of the bed, but she's still alive, trying desperately to hold onto her life. I stalk over to her and grab a handful of her greasy red hair. Slamming her head down, I connect it with the corner of the end table, ending her misery early. Her skull cracks and she'll be dead in seconds. If I had more time or if I didn't have my daughter in my arms, I would've tortured her.

Turns out, I'm a family man now.

Torture can't happen at every enemy encounter. Sometimes I need to be quick and efficient to get back to what's important.

"Let's go see Mommy now," I coo to Zoe. "Daddy's here. No need to be upset."

Zoe grabs my shirt and screams, still super pissed at being slapped, screamed at, and then dropped. Fuck, I'd be pissed too. Holding her to me, I step outside the door I kicked in and frown when I see Adrian's SUV rammed into the unit beside this one. Talia is sitting behind the wheel looking every bit like a mafia queen. Wild eyes. Furious stare. Protective motherly aura rippling toward me in hot waves.

"What did you do to my fuckin' car, woman?" Adrian gripes as he comes up behind me.

"I stayed in the car!" she yells out. "I obeyed! Now bring me my baby!"

Zoe screams harder and tries to flip out of my grip.

Someone wants their mother.

chapter
twenty

Talia

MY FIRST THOUGHT WHEN I SAW KOSTAS STALKING toward the SUV with our baby in his arms was that she's alive and safe and I can finally breathe again. My second thought was how fucking sexy my husband looked holding our daughter to his chest like she's his entire world. Those hands that are capable of killing and torturing are also capable of being gentle and loving. When his eyes met mine, I could see the hardness in his light eyes—quite the contradiction—but the moment he looked down at Zoe, who was crying, his eyes went soft. The same way they go soft when he looks at me.

Once I stop staring at his eyes, and how precious our little girl looks in his arms, I notice the blood. Blood everywhere. All over their clothes, and splattered across their flesh.

"Is that blood?" I jump out of the driver's seat and run around the back, needing to get to Zoe and Kostas. "Is she bleeding?" I snatch her out of Kostas's hands and start checking her for injury. Her face is red and swollen from crying and there's a handprint mark on her thigh, but there're no cuts.

"It's not hers," Kostas says. "We're both okay."

"Who the fuck slapped her?" I bring her thigh up to show him. I'm seeing red. I don't see Selene or Aris anywhere. Did those fuckers touch my baby and then leave her here? That blood better be theirs.

"Selene did," Kostas says through a growl, his jaw tightening.

"Please tell me that bitch is alive," I hiss. "I'm going to fucking kill her."

Kostas shakes his head. "She's dead."

"Did she at least suffer?" I rub my daughter's thigh while holding her close to my chest. Her crying is already calming down.

"This is her blood," Kostas tells me. "I made sure that bitch was in pain before I ended her life."

"And what about Aris?" I glance around, suddenly realizing we've only been discussing Selene.

"He wasn't here," Adrian says.

"What?" I screech. Zoe jumps in my arms, and I remind myself I need to stay calm. "He can be anywhere." My gaze flits around us, hating that we're standing outside. He could be about to pounce.

"We're going to find him," Kostas promises. "Right now, we need to get our daughter home."

Kostas is right. Zoe's diaper is filled to the brim and leaking. She probably has a diaper rash. Who the hell knows when she was fed last. If that bitch wasn't already dead, I would torture and kill her my fucking self. Aris better run far because when I get my hands on him, I'm going to make sure he suffers for the both of them.

"We need to find a hotel," I tell the men as we climb into the SUV. Luckily, when I drove into the front of the building, hoping to create a diversion, the siding was rotted wood and no major damage was done. "We need to get her diapers and clothes and formula. She can't go two hours like this. I need to give her a bath."

The heaviness of everything that's happened is hitting me like a two-ton weight on my chest, and it's hard to breathe. "We need to get her to a doctor," I say through a sob. "What if…what if they hurt her?" I'm supposed to put Zoe in her car seat, but I can't let her out of my arms. She's clinging to me like a little koala bear.

Kostas tells Adrian to stop at the store, and while he runs in to grab stuff for Zoe, Kostas calls a local hotel and makes a reservation. The entire time, Zoe's tiny, chubby arms are wrapped around me with her face snuggled into my chest.

Oh, God, I finally have her back in my arms.

My heart is racing.

I need to get her as far away as possible. To somewhere safe.

What if Aris is following us? Waiting to make his move. What if this is all a trap?

I'm so tired, and all I want to do is snuggle up with my baby, but I need to make sure she's safe.

As I watch her, I notice she's fighting sleep. She's probably too scared. Whatever those pieces of shit did to her has my baby too scared to let herself go to sleep.

When we arrive at the hotel, Adrian checks us in and then both men flank me as we ride the elevator to the top floor. Only my husband would book the Presidential suite when we're only going to be here for a couple hours.

Adrian remains outside, while Kostas and I head

inside. While I give Zoe a bath, checking to make sure there's nothing visibly wrong with her, Kostas rinses off as well. Adrian must've gotten him clothes because when he gets out, he's in a plain white T-shirt and a pair of gray sweatpants.

Once they're both cleaned up, I sit on the couch with Zoe while Kostas makes her a bottle. I hold her close and take in her sweet baby scent, thankful to have her back in my arms.

Her eyes are almost closed at this point, most likely exhausted from everything she's been through, but she's still fighting to stay awake.

My strong fighter. Just like her daddy.

The second the bottle touches her lips, she sucks it down. Her eyes begin to droop, and her stiff body loosens in my arms.

"She was so hungry," I mumble, trying hard to stay strong for my daughter, but inside I'm a mess.

Something worse could've happened to her.

We could've lost her.

"She's a baby," Kostas says. "She'll soon forget what they did to her." He runs his fingers through her head of soft dark curls.

"I'll never forget," I tell him.

And I won't.

Not until the day I die.

Every thought in my being is fueled by the urge to hunt Aris down and punish him for this.

For putting my baby in harm's way.

One day we're going to find him, and when we do. I will make him pay.

"As soon as we get home, we're going to get shit

organized and find Aris," Kostas promises. His words hit me. *Home.* The hotel. The villa where Zoe was taken. The thought of bringing her back there has my heart racing.

"I can't go back there," I blurt out, and Kostas's eyes widen. "I know it's your home, but…"

"*Our* home," Kostas growls out without letting me finish.

"Kostas…"

"If the next words out of your mouth are to tell me you're leaving me, so help me fucking God." Kostas stands, towering over me. Zoe's bottle is empty and she's sleeping soundly in my arms. "You're my fucking wife, and that's our daughter, and if you think I'm going to let you leave me, you better think twice," Kostas chokes out. "I know I fucked up, Talia. Her getting taken is on me." He pounds his fist against his chest, and his eyes bore into mine. "But you aren't fucking leaving me. Ever."

"Kostas, that's not what I was going to say." I consider laying Zoe down, but I can't do it. So instead I stand, still holding her, and walk over to him. "I'm not going anywhere without you."

Kostas's shoulders drop slightly in relief. "Tell me what you need, *zoí mou.*"

"A place where we'll feel safe. A home where Aris hasn't touched and soiled. Maybe one with a pool, so I can take Zoe swimming. But it needs to be secure so nobody gets to us." I just need a damn break. A moment to be at peace with my family without living in fear. It can be months or years before we find Aris, and the hotel no longer feels like my safe place since it's where he stole our daughter. There's no way I'm going to be able to sleep at night, knowing that's where she was taken from.

"I'll handle it," Kostas assures me, already pulling his phone out. "Why don't you and Zoe go lie down and rest and once she wakes up, we'll head out."

Before I head to the room, I step closer to Kostas, and with Zoe sleeping between us, give him a soft kiss. "I don't blame you for any of this. Never think that. I blame Aris and Selene."

Kostas nods once, but I can tell by the way his eyes flinch slightly, he'll always in some way blame himself for not keeping Zoe safe. And I get it, because I'll always blame myself as well.

When we pull up to the house—no, house isn't the right word, more like castle—Kostas gets out and unbuckles Zoe. She's awake now and goes willingly with him. Unlike where Aris kept us, this place is backed up to the beach. I can smell the salt and hear the waves. My heart already feels steadier. My body already feeling lighter.

Surrounding the home is a tall block wall with a wrought iron fence running along the top. From what I can tell, it runs around the entire perimeter of the property. The house is at least three stories tall.

"Nobody is getting in or out of here without my knowledge," Kostas says. "The home is owned by a well-known politician. It's equipped with cameras and has a surveillance room. Once Adrian sets it all up, we'll be able to see every inch of this place right from our phones. And those fences"—he points to the walls—"they're wired with five thousand volts of electricity. One touch and it will knock a person the fuck out."

"Thank you," I tell him, feeling like the weights have been removed from my chest and I can finally breathe again.

"Let's go inside."

The inside is completely furnished. Beautiful shades of cream and bright blue. White wash wood everywhere, giving the entire place an upscale beachy vibe. To the left is a huge living room and dining room—a massive floor-to-ceiling fireplace separating the two. To the right, from what I can tell, is the kitchen. In the middle is a stunning white wash spiral staircase that leads to the upstairs.

"Can we stay here forever?" I joke.

Kostas doesn't laugh, though. "If you want to."

My head whips around to face him. "Are you serious?"

"If this is where you'll feel safe, then it's yours." He shrugs like it's no big deal, when it is in fact a huge deal. This house must cost millions, and he'll buy it just because I love it.

It doesn't matter what I ask for, he always makes sure I get what I want. He said it in his vows that he would make sure I'm always happy, and while I didn't believe them at the time, I know now he meant them. Even back then, when we barely knew each other, he was promising to put my happiness first.

Before I can say anything back, the front door opens and in walks Mom, Stefano, and Phoenix.

"Oh, *miei cari*," Mom cries out. *My darlings.* She runs straight toward Zoe and me and wraps her arms around us. "I was so worried," she cries, which makes me cry.

"We're okay, Mom. Zoe is okay."

Zoe wiggles in my arms and her bright blue eyes pop open. She grants my mom the most beautiful gummy smile, and Mom's and my tears fall even harder.

"Da-da-da," she coos, and Kostas laughs. Of course the only sound she's still making sounds like *Dad*.

"She already knows who she needs to call to get whatever she needs," Kostas says, taking her from me and holding her to his chest.

I sigh, watching him whisper something to our daughter. I don't think I will ever tire of watching him hold her.

"This house is gorgeous," Mom says. "How long are you staying here?"

"Until we find Aris," I tell her at the same time Kostas says, "As long as Talia wants."

We spend the day by the pool—yes, the house has a stunning infinity pool and Jacuzzi—enjoying Zoe. Kostas frequently takes calls, no doubt determined to find Aris. For the first time in months I feel safe and don't even bother to ask him for updates. I'm simply content living in this temporary bubble.

For dinner, Kostas has one of his men pick up groceries and Stefano grills burgers while my mom and I make the side dishes. Everything feels so normal. I know being with Kostas means nothing will ever really be normal, and there will always be threats. My husband is a powerful man who runs a dangerous organization. But seeing another side to him today—him sitting on the lounge chair in his swim trunks, eating a burger and baked beans, and swimming in the pool with Zoe—gives me hope that after we find and kill Aris, we will be able to finally start our life as a family.

After dinner, everyone leaves, and it's only Kostas, Zoe, and me. While we were out back, he of course had her furniture brought over. Her room is upstairs, directly next to ours, but he also had a portable crib put in our room for now.

"Thank you for putting a crib in here." I lay Zoe in her

bed. "It's going to take some time until I'm comfortable with her sleeping in her own room." She's been fed, has a fresh diaper, and is sucking on her pacifier, already half asleep.

"She'll stay with us until you're ready," Kostas says. "But I promise you, she's safe in this house." He locks our bedroom door. "Come shower with me."

When I give him a look, silently asking why he locked our door, he says, "I want to make sure none of my men accidently walk in and see my sexy wife naked. Then I'll have to kill them."

I laugh even though I believe he really would do just that.

With my hand in his, he guides us into the bathroom. From here, we can still see Zoe's crib.

I watch as he pushes his trunks down his muscular thighs, and his thick cock springs free. His eyes meet mine, and the love that shines in them takes my breath away. I've always thought Kostas was sexy, but seeing him as a father, interacting with our daughter, makes him beautiful. And when he looks at me the way he is right now, knowing that underneath all that darkness is a lightness only reserved for Zoe and me to see, makes my heart swell.

I strip out of my bikini, keeping my eyes on Kostas as his heated gaze runs over every inch of my body. If looks could burn, I would be on fire.

"Come here, wife," he demands. He turns the water on and steps into the shower first. There are several showerheads raining down on us, so no matter where we stand warm water hits us.

"How are you feeling?" he asks, framing my cheeks with his strong hands. Our bodies are flush against one another, and he has me backed up against the wall.

"I'm good," I tell him honestly. My eyes flit out of the open shower and into our bedroom, thankful I can see Zoe. "I'm not sure I'll ever be able to let her out of my sight."

"Does that mean when she's a teenager, we can keep her locked up?" Kostas asks, his lips twitching in amusement. I love every side of him. The serious, the sweet, the silly.

"Don't rush my baby growing up." I pout, and Kostas grins.

With his thumb and finger on my chin, he tilts my head up and his lips descend on mine. My arms cling to his neck as our mouths tangle and our tongues duel with one another. Tasting. Coaxing. Getting lost in each other. I didn't realize how much I needed his touch, to feel him until now. We kiss until the water turns cold, and then after quickly washing our bodies, Kostas carries me out of the shower.

With both of us dripping wet, he sets me on the sink and spreads my thighs. His mouth goes right back to mine, his tongue massaging mine. His hands grip my hips, and he pulls me toward him. My hot center rubs against his pelvis. My fingers wrap around his hard shaft, and I stroke it, getting it hard, before I guide it into me.

Kostas's mouth leaves mine to watch as he enters me slowly, filling me with every inch of him. We both watch as we become one. When I'm filled to the hilt with him, he pulls out slowly.

"Do you see this?" he asks, already knowing I do. "Your cunt was made just for me." My insides tighten at his dirty words, and he smirks. He pushes himself back into me, hitting my G-spot.

"Faster," I beg, desperate to find my release. My breasts are heavy and my nipples are painfully erect. I need more, but he's refusing to give it to me.

"There's no rush, *moró mou*," he purrs, continuing to push in and out slowly. Every time he enters me, the head of his cock hits me deep. Little by little, like a hurricane on the horizon, my orgasm builds higher and higher. With every thrust, I can feel it getting closer, gaining momentum.

Kostas finds my clit, and he massages it in circles, still watching as he enters me deeply and then draws out slowly. In and out. Bringing me to the precipice and then taking me away from the edge before I can fall.

"Kostas, please," I beg. Can one die from being denied an orgasm? I'd rather not find out.

When his eyes meet mine, his gaze is filled with lust and love. Heat and desire. My back arches slightly, and my breasts are thrust in his face. He takes a nipple between his lips, and when he bites down on it, my body convulses in pleasure.

His thumb leaves my clit, and he cages me in, somehow filling me even deeper than before. That's all it takes for my body to detonate. His mouth covers mine, muffling my screams of pleasure as he drives into me. My hips rise to meet his thrust for thrust as we both come completely undone.

My legs are shaking, and my body has gone limp. It takes a few minutes to calm my heavy breathing. Kostas pulls out of me and smirks at what I'm sure is his cum dripping between my legs. There's no doubt he's going to have me knocked up soon…and I can't fucking wait.

chapter
twenty-one

Kostas

"Y
OU KNOW WHAT? FUCK HIM." I SCRUB MY
palm down my face before leveling Adrian
with a hard glare. "I'm done going after him.
It's what he wants."

"No," Adrian argues. "What he wants is to toy with you."

It's been days since we rescued our daughter. Days since
we've used up all our energy looking for my brother. I'm over
it, dammit.

"With what resources?" I demand. "I get that he could
do that shit when he had access to the Demetriou fortune.
When he had a bitch who worshiped the ground he walked
on. When he had a fucking car. But now? He has fucking
nothing. I'm done wasting precious time with my family to
hunt down this motherfucker."

"I'll have Basil continue to probe his contacts. Just because you don't want to actively search for him doesn't mean
we can't still keep an eye out for him," Adrian says.

A year ago, I would've fucked over a man with just my
knife if he'd undermined my authority. Now, I think a little

differently. Besides, Adrian means well and has my best interest at heart.

"You got anyone besides Basil?" I ask, irritation clipping my tone.

Adrian's brows knit together. I know they're like brothers, but brothers can fucking turn on you. I of all people know this. "Wesley is there. He's one of my best and most trusted."

"Give Wesley the same job. Then, we can compare notes on what information they give back to us."

Adrian is clearly annoyed, but he nods before texting. While he busies himself with the affairs of the dark side of my business, I have to deal with the legit side. I call and make arrangements with the hotel manager, Carla. She'll get started on hiring a construction crew to repair the damage Aris and Selene inflicted upon the hotel while also updating some areas of the hotel that need it. We'll be down for the season, but our other hotels in Crete and Santorini will bring in plenty of profit.

"Where's Phoenix?" I ask once he's done firing off messages.

"Last I saw, he was out by the pool with the girls."

I exit my office and make my way to the back door. As I exit, one of the men, Fowler, bows his head in respect. Phoenix stands by the pool like a sentry, looking more formidable than the five guards I have placed all over the backyard. He's dressed in a suit that fits his style unlike that shitty stuff he and his father always wore. It's like he belongs here. And I know he'd do anything to protect Talia.

Which makes him perfect for what I need him for.

Pushing through the door, I nod to him before walking over to the edge of the pool. Melody waves to me from a pool lounger. I crouch to give my wife a kiss and to grin at my daughter. She lets out a squeal of laughter, melting away all my anger and irritation. If I didn't have so much shit to do, I'd go swimming with them. But, even bad guys have to fucking work.

"My beautiful girls," I say before leaving them to play. I click my tongue and nod into the house, motioning for Phoenix to follow me. "Watch them," I bark out to Fowler.

"Always, sir," Fowler says back.

As soon as we're in my office with Adrian, I close the door and pull out the ouzo. I'm not the lush I once was, but now that I have my family back, I can relax with a drink from time to time. I make the three of us a drink and then settle in my office chair. Phoenix is guarded but stoic. I study him for a long while and decide that both he and Talia have Melody's strength. I tapped into her strength when Talia was missing, so I know this firsthand. With Niles gone, it's easier to note the similarities between the siblings. He's lucky. The fucker is growing on me. Talia sure as hell did.

"Your duties in Thessaloniki are over." I sip my ouzo and watch for his reaction.

His jaw ticks, but he doesn't show anger. "Is that so?"

"It is." I reach into my drawer and pull out a set of keys. "The Land Rover in the garage is yours. Trade it in for what you want."

He lifts a brow. "Okay. You going to elaborate?"

"Your father is dead. Your sister is here. What more do you want?"

"Not bullshit answers," he grumbles, frowning just like my fucking wife.

I let out a heavy sigh. "My brother betrayed me. You'd

die for your sister. I need someone like that on my team. Someone who would give up anything to protect my wife. Is that someone you?"

"You want a Nikolaides to come work for a Demetriou?" He scoffs, shaking his head. "Never thought I'd see the day."

Adrian snorts out a laugh. We never saw this coming either. But here we are.

"Technically, you already did work for us in case you've forgotten," I grit out. "Again, are you willing to trade your glorious life back in Thessaloniki for one on Crete Island? You'll be paid handsomely."

"Like I've ever given a fuck about the money," he bites out. "All I care about is my family."

"Then that will be your reward, Phoenix. You'll have unlimited access to both my wife and my daughter. I'll bring you into the fold—erase your fucking Nikolaides past, and give you a Demetriou future. But once you're in, there's no getting out."

He leans back in his chair and gulps down his ouzo before setting the glass down hard. "What do you want me to do? Guard my sister?"

As much as I would love that added layer of protection, I need Phoenix for more.

"You've handled the taxes quite nicely. You have a flair for numbers, correct?"

He nods. "Dad sure as hell didn't. I learned at an early age how to run numbers to help his ass out."

"Good. I've just lost my numbers man." My chair creaks when I lean forward, placing my elbows on my desk and steepling my fingers. "The moment you're given the key to the castle, there is no turning back. If I even sniff one ounce of you turning coat, I will fucking destroy you, Phoenix. I will make Talia cut into you and remove each organ for me. Are we clear?"

Adrian laughs again, earning a scowl from Phoenix.

"You're such a fucking psychopath," he grumbles. "And, no, I'd never do that shit to my sister. You have my word."

"Wonderful. Now run along and go trade that expensive ass car in for another stupid Jeep. We have to go over a mountain of shit. The sooner you get back, the sooner we can get to it." I wave him off with a flick of my hand.

Phoenix rises and gives Adrian an incredulous look. "Does he talk to you like that?"

"He grows on you," Adrian says with a snort.

"Right," Phoenix grumbles. He stops mid stride and turns to glower at me, making me tense. "And Jeeps aren't stupid. They're practical."

Adrian laughs. "Go on, boy, before you get bitch slapped."

"You assholes can fucking try," Phoenix says with a smirk that reminds me of Talia. Ornery fucker.

As soon as he's gone, I pull up my laptop and dive back into business, both legit and nefarious. A villain's work is never done.

I wake up in the dead of the night to my phone ringing off the hook.

"What?" I snarl into the line.

"Your father's place," Adrian barks out. "I'm on my way. Meet me there."

He hangs up on me. What the fuck? I slide out of bed and start throwing on clothes.

"Where are you going?" Talia asks, her voice raspy from sleep.

I lean over the bed and kiss her mouth. "Business. Phoenix and the men will be here. Your gun is in your bedside table. Use it if you need to."

As I start to pull away, she grabs my wrist. "I love you."

"Love you too."

Within five minutes, I'm dressed and locking the bedroom door behind me. I stalk down the hallway to the guest room where Phoenix is staying before pushing inside. When I flick on the lights, he snags his Glock and has it aimed in my direction. Good reflexes.

"Need you to keep an eye on Talia and Zoe. Something's happened at my father's place," I tell him before turning on my heel.

He pads behind me. "Another diversion?"

I stalk into the spare room where we have a gun safe and turn the dial on the lock. "I don't know, but we can never be too sure. Just in case"—I toss him an AR-15—"use brute force to protect them."

In nothing but boxers and socks, Phoenix still manages to look formidable with a Glock in one hand and the AR in the other.

"You think he's coming out of hiding?" he asks.

"Nah," I grunt as I push past him. "He's just fucking with me. It's what he does."

"He'll slip up one day, Kostas," Phoenix calls out after me. "And we'll make him fucking pay."

"Damn right we will."

The drive to my father's is quick as our new home isn't

too far from there. I'm less than a mile away when I see what the fuck happened. That asshole set our childhood home on fire. I push back memories of my mother and me in the kitchen. Many nights when I was small and she'd read stories about heroes to me. The scent of her perfume that still lingered even a year after her death.

Fuck Aris.

It was his mother too.

This just proves to me he's nothing but a sociopath. All he cares about is number one. Himself. And his favorite way of pleasuring himself is to fuck with me. Sick bastard.

By the time I reach the home, it's completely engulfed in flames. The firefighters are already doing their best to control the fire so it doesn't spread elsewhere. I pull up next to Adrian's SUV and hop out.

"What the hell?" I snap, trotting over to him.

He scowls at me. "Aris."

"No fucking shit."

"And, Boss…" He pinches the bridge of his nose. "I can't get ahold of Basil."

My blood runs cold. "It's the middle of the night. Understandable."

"Wesley says he never came back to the hotel last night."

"Aris took him?"

Adrian's features pinch. "He packed his shit, man."

A rat. I had a hunch before and I was right. Unfuckingbelievable.

"Put Wesley in charge at the hotel. I want you on point hunting Basil down."

"I thought we were done hunting," Adrian huffs, irritation making his voice gruff.

"Aris. Basil is a different story. We find Basil, we'll find

Aris. Find out where the fuck he went, when he went there, and why he thought fucking me over was a smart plan. We find Basil, and I'll bleed out every detail he knows about Aris."

Adrian scowls but nods. "Yep."

I clutch his shoulder and give it a squeeze. "Brothers can turn. But you and I? We don't fucking turn. You feel me, Adrian? We're better than brothers."

"I'm gonna find his ass and haul him in myself. This shit will end soon," he vows. The exhaustion from this entire Aris debacle over the past year has worn down on my longtime friend.

As soon as he gets in his SUV and leaves, I pull up my security cameras. Talia is asleep in the bed and she's moved Zoe with her. Phoenix paces the hallway right outside their door dressed all in black, the AR slung over his shoulder. Thank fuck. The rest of the men are stationed around the perimeter of my house. At least they're safe.

But they won't be until I deal with my fuckface brother.

I'm going to find his crazy ass and end him because I'm getting too old for this shit. Can't a man just settle the fuck down and have one goddamn week to be a normal fucking husband and father?

Until I drag Aris's ass into that cellar, I won't.

I need to start thinking like him. If I were Aris, what the hell would I do next to fuck with me? Cars are a dime a dozen. He doesn't know the location of our new home. That leaves the hotel. I text Adrian to secure the property from every angle. Next, I text Josef.

Me: I want every cop hunting down Aris Demetriou. Every fucking one of them.
Josef: And compensation?

Me: Money. Lots of it.

Josef: And?

Me: Reelection.

Josef: Done.

If Josef leads me to Aris, I'll get him into any political position he so fucking desires. My next text is to a low-level punk gangster with a big mouth—someone I pay to get messages out.

Me: Aris Demetriou to me alive. 50 mil. Spread the word.

Jaws: Poppy needs a new pair of shoes. On it, Boss.

I don't care if my brother drains me dry. I'd gladly lose every dime if it means having him strapped to a chair in the cellar. Every goddamn dime. Because once he's dead, I'll just make more fucking money. I'm a Demetriou. It's what we do.

chapter
twenty-two

Talia

"GUESS WHAT TODAY IS?" I ASK ZOE AS I PICK her up out of her crib. She flails her chubby arms and babbles like crazy, excited to see me.

Last night was the first night in her own room and I swear I got up thirty times throughout the night to check on her. I know she needs to sleep in her own room, but it's hard to be away from her.

With Aris having burned down their family home recently, Kostas has our home on lockdown. Nobody is allowed to come or go except for him and his men. Stefano had to leave for Italy to get back to work, but my mom has extended her stay. Thankfully, we have a beautiful pool house, complete with its own kitchen and laundry room, so while she's here, she's staying there.

"What's today?" Kostas asks, stepping behind me. I lay Zoe across her changing table so I can change her diaper and get her dressed.

"Today, Miss Zoe is seven months old." I lean over and

blow raspberries on her belly. Her giggles ring out through the room. "Every month when I lived with…" I stop myself, not wanting to bring up Kostas's brother. With Aris still missing and wreaking havoc all over town, Kostas's frustration has been at an all-time high. The last thing I want to do is add to that.

"What?" he prompts.

"Never mind. She's seven months old today, that's all."

"Talia." He picks Zoe up from the changing table then turns to face me. "Whatever happened while we were apart, I want to know. It fucking kills me that I missed out on everything. Your pregnancy, Zoe's birth, the first six months of her life…"

He's right. I can't help what happened while I was being held captive by Aris. And stopping my tradition just because it began while I was at Aris's house only gives him power he doesn't deserve.

"I started a tradition when Zoe turned a month old. I would bake cupcakes and after dinner, I would light a candle in one and make a wish. Then afterward, I would take our picture. I would make Aris get it printed and I put each one into a scrap book."

Kostas smiles softly. "What did you wish for?"

"For you to find us." I take a breath, not wanting to cry. I started my period this morning, so I know I'm being overly emotional. We're home and safe, and there's no reason to cry.

Kostas steps toward me and pushes a wayward strand of hair out of my face. "Looks like this month you'll have to make a new wish." He bends slightly and kisses me. It's sweet and quick, but it still lights my belly on fire.

"Do you still have the scrapbook?" he asks.

"I do. I snatched it when I grabbed our stuff."

"You'll have to show it to me," he insists.

When he steps back, I notice he's dressed in his suit. "Are you leaving?"

"I need to handle a few things at the office. Handle my parents' house."

"Will it be able to be saved?"

"No, but it was fully insured. I need to meet with the agent today to go over everything." He gives Zoe a kiss, then hands her to me. "I should be home for dinner. Save me a cupcake." He winks playfully, and I laugh at how damn sexy he is when he's playful.

After seeing him out, I head into the kitchen to make the cupcakes. My mom comes in as I'm setting them in the oven with a cup of coffee in her hand.

"Did you sleep okay?" I ask, grabbing my own cup of coffee and sitting at the table across from her. Zoe is sitting in her high chair, playing with her new sippy cup and eating her cheerios.

"I slept very well." She smiles. "That bed is so comfortable. I'm going to have to tell Stefano to buy us one." She glances into the kitchen. "Baking this early?"

"They're Zoe's seven-month cupcakes. I make them every month to celebrate her birthday."

Mom grins from ear to ear. "Kind of like your birthday pancakes?"

"Yeah." I laugh, remembering when I was growing up I would insist Mom make pancakes like every day. Not wanting to make them all the time, she would say they were only for special occasions. So, every time I would ask, I would make up an excuse, like it was my twelve-year, two-month birthday. She could've totally told me I was full of shit, but she never did. Instead, she would make them every time.

"How's Kostas doing?" she asks. I hate that I was gone for over a year, but I love that something good came from the shitty situation. A friendship of sorts was formed between Kostas and my mom. And not just between them, but also between Kostas and Phoenix. Well, maybe not a friendship between Kostas and Phoenix per se…but definitely a mutual understanding. Kostas even gave him a job and a place to live at the hotel.

"He's okay. Just stressed. Aris is still missing, and instead of keeping quiet, he's apparently trying to create destruction at every turn to bring Kostas down."

"Has he done anything else since he burned down their parents' home?"

"Last night they think he tried to burn the hotel down. Some wires got tripped, but Kostas was ready for him and they caught it quickly, so no damage was done. But, of course, they didn't see who did it. So, now Kostas thinks there's a rat."

Mom huffs in disgust. "I hope they catch him soon."

"Same, but until they do, I think it's safe to say Kostas will be on edge. I just wish there was something I could do."

Mom takes a sip of her coffee and when she sets it down, she grins. "What if I take Zoe to the pool house with me tonight, so you can make him a romantic dinner? You can spend some time just the two of you."

My first thought is there's no way I'm letting Zoe out of my sight, but then, after I take a deep breath, I remember the pool house is only a few yards away and my mom did raise me. She's great with Zoe.

"I'll even ask Phoenix to come over," she adds, obviously sensing my reluctance. "I can spend some time with my son and granddaughter, and you can have a nice, peaceful dinner with your husband."

The buzzer goes off, indicating the cupcakes are done, so I head over to the oven and take them out.

"What do you think?" she prompts.

"I think that would be great." I open the fridge to see what we have. Upon inspection, I find I have everything I need to make Kostas's favorite: chicken parmesan.

"But not overnight," I tell her. "Once we're done, I'm coming to get my baby back."

She laughs and shakes her head. "It's so hard to believe that *my* baby is all grown up." She stands and walks over to me, enveloping me in one of her comforting hugs. "You've grown into such a beautiful woman, Talia," she says. "A loving mother and a devoted wife. I'm so proud of you."

"Thank you, Mom." That means a lot coming from her because she's not only my mom, but my best friend, and growing up, I always wanted to be just like her.

After cleaning up the kitchen, we get changed into our swimsuits and head out to the pool. It's a perfectly sunny day with not a cloud in sight.

While Mom holds Zoe, I swim some laps, and once I'm done, I take Zoe around in her little inflatable boat that has an umbrella top on it to provide shade. She giggles and splashes in the water. Only getting out of the pool to eat her snacks and drink her juice.

When lunchtime rolls around, I give Zoe back to Mom, so I can grab us something to eat.

"Need help with anything?" a masculine voice asks. Bending to grab my towel, I glance over my shoulder to find Fowler standing right behind me with his gaze pointed directly at my butt.

Since Basil has gone MIA, Kostas and Adrian are out more, so that leaves Fowler and the team watching over us.

189

At first, when I would catch him checking me out, I thought I was seeing things, but the more he does it, the more I realize he's a fucking perv. And a dumbass because once I tell Kostas, he's going to kill him. I almost feel bad.

I stand back up and turn around. "Nope, I got it."

"You sure?" Fowler steps closer and the small hairs on the back of my nape rise.

"Well, if you really want to help, you can start by watching *my family* instead of watching *me.*"

I know he gets what I'm insinuating because he smirks. It's smarmy and sends chills up my spine. I glance around, hoping to see another one of Kostas's men, but it's just us. I know they're all over the grounds, but only one usually stays with us inside the house or out back.

"Sorry, I'm a flirt by nature. Nothing meant by it." He shrugs, not even bothering to look guilty, despite his words, for staring at my body. "It's hard to focus when you're dressed like that." He grins boyishly and nods toward me. I'm wearing a two-piece bikini, and sure, it might be on the small side, but I'm in my own home, and even if I weren't, I should be able to wear whatever the hell I want without being ogled by Kostas's men.

Just as I'm about to give this asshole a piece of my mind, I hear my husband call out my name.

Perfect timing.

"*Moró mou,*" Kostas says, pulling me into his side. He kisses my temple then addresses Fowler. "How's everything?"

Fowler's gaze flits from me back to Kostas and I swear I see a hint of a smirk playing on the corner of his lips. *Does this guy seriously want to die?* "Absolutely perfect," he says.

"Kostas, can I talk to you for a minute?" I ask.

"Of course." He turns his attention back to me.

When Fowler doesn't take the hint, I add, "Alone."

Kostas's brows knit together. "What's the matter, Talia? If there's an issue, Fowler needs to know as well. Did something happen?"

"No, nothing happened." I glance over at Fowler, who's still standing there, with his arms crossed over his chest, and his eyes roaming my body. Is this guy for real? "Well, actually something did happen." I look pointedly at Fowler. "This guy keeps checking me out, and it's making me uncomfortable."

Kostas's brows dip further. "Is this true?" he asks Fowler. "Are you checking out my wife?"

"Sir, it wasn't like that," Fowler sputters. His back goes straight, and finally, his eyes are no longer on me.

"Either you did or you didn't check my wife out. It's simple."

"She's wearing a skimpy bikini, sir, and I might've noticed. I didn't mean any offense."

I scoff at the way he's downplaying this. He was totally perving on me.

"Where's Greg?" Kostas asks him.

"In the security room," Fowler says.

"And Kip?"

"Guarding the front."

Kostas steps toward Fowler, and since Kostas is a good half a foot taller, he looks down at him. "I don't give a fuck if my wife is naked, you don't ever look at her in any way other than to make sure she's safe. Understand?" His voice is calm, but I can see it in the way his jaw is ticking, he's about to lose his shit.

Good! Serves that asshole right.

"Yes, sir," Fowler says like the good soldier he is. Gag.

"Go take over for Kip and tell him to get back here."

What? That's it? He's just assigning him to a different location?

After Fowler leaves, Kostas's eyes swing back over to me. "Talia, is that the only bathing suit you have?"

Oh, no, he didn't.

"No, but—"

"Go change into something more appropriate, please."

I glance over at my mom, who is lying on a chaise lounge with Zoe in her arms. I can tell by the look on her face she can hear everything that's happening.

"I'm not changing," I tell Kostas, crossing my arms over my chest in defiance. "This is my home, and I'll wear whatever the hell I want."

Kostas's brows rise in shock. "Talia, it wasn't a suggestion. Go fucking change. I'm not going to have you prancing around here so my men can ogle what's mine."

What's his? Like I'm a goddamn piece of property!

"You're a chauvinist pig, and if you don't walk away right now, I'm going to push your ass into that pool." I walk around Kostas and over to Mom. I take Zoe out of her hands, so I can lay her down for a nap.

"Talia," Kostas growls, but I ignore him, because if I don't, we're going to fight. And I'm choosing to chalk his dumb ass remarks up to stress because of Aris.

"I'll see you tonight!" I call out behind me.

"So, that's it?" he shouts back. When I keep walking, he says, "Real fucking nice, Talia. I'm so glad I came home to see my family for lunch."

Too pissed, and afraid I'll say something I might regret later, I don't bother answering him. And the smart man he is, doesn't follow me.

While I'm laying Zoe down, I think about everything

he said. While he's in the wrong, he also made a valid point about being appropriate in front of his men. Not wanting to fight with him over something so trivial, when I get back downstairs, I look for him to apologize, but he's already gone. Great, now I'm going to need to make sure this dinner is extra perfect because if I know my husband, he's going to come home cranky as hell later.

Chicken Parmesan-check.

Pasta and sauce-check.

Salads-check.

Wine-check.

Oh! The bread.

Remembering I placed it in the warmer, I run back into the kitchen to grab it. Since my mom has Zoe, and I'm making this dinner for Kostas, I frosted Zoe's cupcakes and put them away. I figure we can make our wish tomorrow. One day won't make a difference. Plus, with Kostas being all growly, I figured the best way to calm him down will be to ply him with his favorite food, since I'm on my period and can't have sex with him. If he's extra cranky, I'll give him head. That always softens him up.

I hear the door open then slam shut, and then Kostas's voice booms throughout the house.

Great, just as I thought…he's cranky.

"I don't give a fuck what he said," he barks into the phone. "I've had enough of this back and forth bullshit. I want answers!"

With the bread basket in my hands, I'm stepping into

the dining room, when I see Kostas already in there. He yells some more at whoever he's on the phone with, and then, like it's happening in slow motion, his fist comes out and swipes at the items on the table. The wine glasses shatter, the chicken parmesan splatters, and the salads fly through the air.

I gape at the destroyed table, my eyes fixated on the red sauce that will stain the wall it's slowly trekking a path down. The entire meal I just spent hours making is completely ruined.

Kostas's eyes meet mine, and he looks around, as if now realizing what he did.

"Talia," he breathes.

"My mom's watching Zoe for us… I made you dinner," I choke out. "And it's ruined." I don't have to feel my cheeks to know I'm crying. I know it's just food, but I worked hard on it to make him feel better and with one swipe, he destroyed it all.

"Shit." He scrubs his hands over his face in frustration. He's always frustrated. Always mad. When he found us, it was supposed to be the beginning of our life together, but instead, because of Aris, it's as if our life is on hold. Kostas tries so hard not to let this side of him show in front of Zoe and me, but I've been watching it build and build, and he's finally reached his boiling point.

"I didn't mean to," he says, stepping toward me, his brow furling and his eyes shining with remorse. "It's just…it's been a bad fucking day."

chapter
twenty-three

Kostas

TALIA RUSHES OFF AND I FEEL LIKE A FUCKING animal. I scrub my palm over my face and laugh bitterly. Aris has infected every part of my relationship with Talia straight from the beginning. He's like a bite from a zombie and as time passes, I'm becoming infected too.

I want to hack him away from me.

Sever him like a diseased limb I'll be better off without.

We're at war, my brother and me, and it's fucking bloody. But I will win.

Winning means keeping my wife happy. Because when we're happy, Aris has lost. The loser in a game where he didn't get the girl. Even when he stole her, she was never his. She will never be his.

I can be pissed as fuck at my brother, but allowing him to creep into our evening time alone and ruin our dinner is too much. He doesn't deserve that win. And my wife deserves more than that.

With a heavy sigh, I clean up the mess. Sure, we have

people to do this, but I need to be the one to do it. To smell the heavenly sauce I won't get to eat. To curse over the expensive bottle of wine that's ruined and never tasted. To face the consequences of my destruction. And to clean it all up.

Talia is next.

I'll kiss her and make it all better.

Once the dining room is cleaned up, I grab a bottle of vodka from the cabinet and set it on the counter. Then, I pull out some salami, several cheeses, crackers, and grapes. After arranging them on a giant plate, I locate the can of leftover frosting in the fridge. Shoving a spoon into the top, I then place it in the center of my plate of apologies. I tuck the vodka under my arm and grab up the plate. I don't find her right away because she's not in our bedroom. Eventually, I locate her in the theater room. Sitting in the dark. Crying. Fuck.

I turn on the lights and she buries her face in her hands. Setting down the plate and alcohol on the table beside a vase filled with fresh Gerber daisies, I pick up the remote to turn on the giant eighty-five-inch screen. It takes some scrolling through Netflix, but I find a version of *Romeo + Juliet* I can handle. Leonardo DiCaprio and Claire Danes. I kick off my shoes and sit down beside her.

"I know you don't want to hear me tell you I'm sorry again," I say softly, gripping her thigh and squeezing. "So I'm not saying it. You don't respond to that shit anyway."

She hisses at me. "Fuck you!" she bellows, kicking out and sending the goddamn vase on the table flying across the room. Her fucking periods will be the death of me.

"What I mean," I growl, staring at yet another broken vase, "is you do better with actions. I made you a charcuterie board."

"You can't win me over with your fancy cheese plate,"

she bites out. "Not after you threw my dinner to the floor, Kostas Demetriou."

I snort, which earns me another hiss from her. "You didn't even look at it."

She peeks out between her fingers that still cover her face. "Is that chocolate icing?"

I'm a smart fucking man.

"I bet the grapes taste good dipped in the chocolate icing," I offer, reaching over to pluck a grape from the vine, and then run it along the fudgy sweetness. "Should I taste it first?"

She pops her lips open like a petulant toddler finally giving in to receiving her medicine. I pretend to put the grape to her mouth, but then replace it with my lips at the last second. Her gasp is one of surprise, and before she can push me away, I nip at her bottom lip.

"I love you," I murmur before finally treating her to the chocolate grape.

"Mmm," she moans, her eyes fluttering closed. "I still hate you, but just a little less."

"Then I better keep feeding you."

"You better."

"I put your favorite movie on," I tell her.

She laughs, but it's a mean laugh that gets my dick hard. "I hate this version."

"But you know all the words," I argue. "Your eyes light up when you watch it."

"It's cheesy," she grumbles.

"I'll show you cheesy."

"Oh my God." She fights a smile as I pile salami and cheese onto a cracker. "You're totally cheesy. This is ridiculous. Twenty minutes ago you were furious and slinging shit around our kitchen. Now you're telling me dumb dad jokes and watching corny chick flicks? This is why I hate you."

"You love me," I explain as I shove the whole cracker in her mouth to keep her quiet so I can speak. "You love me because I am nothing without you."

Her brows crash together as she chomps on the cracker in such an unladylike way it makes me want to lick every single crumb that falls onto her thighs.

"You make me want to be better than I ever thought I could be. I never cared to be *better* until you. Now, this villain thinks he can be your hero." I lean my forehead against hers. "I'm going to be really honest here. I'll suck at it at first. You'll hate me at least once a week. But I'm fucking trying, Talia. For you. For Zoe. For our family."

She swallows and pouts. "You make it sound like I don't appreciate you. I do, even when you're an asshole."

"I see your pretty face and every horrible thing I've ever done is forgotten. All that matters is you and our daughter. I fucking bask in your presence, whether you're beaming at me or burning me with your anger. As long as you're the one doing it, I fucking want it. All the warm, happy moments and the raging, hot terrible ones. You, Talia. I want you."

"I want you too. I hate that we're being deprived of our happiness because of him."

I grip her jaw and kiss her softly. "I'm going to try harder. To leave the stress at the door. By bringing it in our home, I'm letting him win. I'll be damned if I let that weasel win."

"We win," she tells me firmly. "You and me, Kos. We're a team. A filthy king and his adorable queen." She laughs and it sounds like music.

"Accept my apology," I demand, nipping at her bottom lip. "Now, woman."

"You're such a prick," she says with a sigh. "My prick."

I grip her hand and run it over my cock. "Your prick's right here."

"Your prick is being punished," she tells me primly. "Go on. Feed me some more. I'm enjoying the groveling." She leans forward to grab the vodka and makes a seductive show of unscrewing the lid before wrapping her dick sucking lips around the bottle.

With my eyes on her so I don't miss the way her throat bobs as she swallows down the burn, I fix her another cheese and meat cracker. The movie plays in the background—the soundtrack working in my benefit to seduce my wife. As the food disappears and the bottle empties, I warm my woman up. All anger has dissipated as giggles take over.

"What's so funny?" I murmur, my lips tracing kisses along the side of her neck. "Romeo and Juliet is a tragedy."

"This version is," she snorts.

"A man tries to be romantic and this is how he's rewarded." I bite her warm flesh. "Maybe I should stop wooing you and just ravish you instead." When I slide my palm up her bare thigh to just under her dress, she lets out a sharp breath and grips my wrist.

"I'm on my period, remember?"

"So?"

"Kostas!"

"You think I'm afraid of blood?"

"Don't be gross."

"Nothing about fucking you on your period is gross."

She gapes at me when I push her dress up her hips.

"Lie back," I order.

"Kostas…"

I reach under her dress and grip her panties. Her breath hitches when I tug them down her thighs. Once they're tossed away, I kiss up her naked thigh.

"Kostas," she whines. "I have a tampon in. This is weird."

Ignoring her half-ass pleas to get me to stop, I run my tongue up her inner thigh. She moans when I suck on the apex of her thigh. Gripping her knees, I spread her open. The string of her tampon remains within reach, but I leave it alone to seek out her clit.

"I like the way you smell." I lick her clit, loving the way she shudders. "I like the way you taste. You think I was a vampire in another life?"

"Do not go there," she breathes. "Please."

Maybe not today.

There's always next month.

"Can I go here?" I ask, circling her clit with my tongue.

"Y-Yes. Go there. Mmm."

Smiling against her pussy, I tease her bundle of nerves until she's squirming on the sofa. I listen to the sounds of her breathing and pay attention to the way her hips lift each time she gets close to orgasm. When I know she's about to fall over the edge, I suck hard on her clit. She screams in pleasure as her whole body detonates. I press kisses to her perfect pussy as I tug on the string of her tampon.

"What are you doing?" she hisses, her chest heaving.

"This." I gently pull until her body releases the bloody plug. With my eyes searing hers, I drop the thing onto the empty cheese plate and then yank at my belt. Her pussy is open and inviting.

A little blood doesn't fucking scare me.

I'm a goddamn villain.

Blood turns us the hell on.

I unfasten my pants and pull out my aching cock. After I shove my pants down my thighs and rip at the buttons on my shirt, I prowl over to her, deciding that's enough stripping. I want inside her before she changes her mind.

"See this pussy?" I ask, teasing her opening with the tip of my dick.

She nods, frowning.

"It's mine," I growl with a hard thrust of my hips.

My dick slides into her warmth and I groan. Her lips are parted, her eyes soft. I want to fucking devour her. She cries out when my lips crash to hers. I kiss her hard and urgently, making her feel my apologies for what I've done and my hope for how I want to be. She kisses me back, equally as passionate.

Talia meets my fire with gasoline.

She taunts and draws out the beast inside me.

And rather than being fearful of the man I can be, she lets me own her with my mouth and punish her cunt with my cock. Begs and moans for it. Fucking loves it.

The sounds coming from her body are juicier than normal and it makes me hard as stone. It takes everything in me not to come without at least attempting to make her come again. Luckily, my girl is needy and tipsy, and the moment my fingers touch her clit, she clenches around my dick as she yells my name. I thrust into her several more times until my balls draw up, desperate for release. With a groan, I spill my seed in her bloody cunt. What a fucking mess we are. A beautiful mess.

With a peck to her lips, I pull out slowly, loving the way her blood is smeared over my thickness. If I didn't just come, I'd have the urge to wrap my hand around my dick and use her blood as lubricant, bringing myself to climax. Talia fucking undoes my mind.

"I can't believe I let you do that," she complains, but her voice is breathless and happy.

"Believe it. Because in about five minutes, I'm going to regroup and do it again in the shower."

"It blew up last night."

You've got to be fucking kidding me.

"Planes don't just blow up," I growl to Adrian. "Fucking Aris. What did airport security say?"

"They're investigating and looking through video footage to see what happened."

"We know what happened. Aris wanted to fuck around with me."

He lets out a heavy sigh. "I'll look into it. But good news is, I have a lead."

"Oh?"

"Wesley said the vehicle Basil took had less than a quarter tank of gas."

I lean back in my office chair. "And?"

"And all the service stations have been checked. He never arrived to refuel."

"So it means Basil is close. Aris is close."

"Any hideouts within fifty miles or so?" he asks. "I could start checking in on some."

We pretty much own everything worth owning within that radius. My mind flits to a few motels that we don't. One particular shithole is known for shady motherfuckers staying at. It would be stupid for Aris to go there, especially with a fifty-mil price tag for his head, but that doesn't mean he wouldn't try it.

"Let's check it out," I order.

After a quick kiss to Talia and Zoe who are napping, I grab my keys. I find Phoenix in a heated discussion with Fowler, but I don't stick around to break it up. Phoenix has taken command over these men, so if Fowler with the wandering fucking eyes needs an attitude adjustment, who am I to step in and interfere.

Adrian and I climb into my Maserati before zipping through town toward the shitty motel. Fifteen minutes later, we creep up to the building. On the side, a vehicle is parked with a blue tarp covering it.

"Basil's car," Adrian growls, jumping from my car before I get it in park.

We didn't have a plan coming here, just following yet another lead. Most leads are pointless. It's surprising as fuck this one might lead us right to Aris.

"I want at him before you kill him," Adrian hisses over his shoulder. "Give me that. I want to ask him straight to his face why he'd turn on his best friend."

I follow him along the sidewalk. We creep, listening in at each door. Nothing seems of interest until I hear him. Moaning. Lifting my leg, I kick in the door hard. Adrian rushes past me, his gun drawn. When he stops suddenly, I slam into his back.

"What the fu—" My jaw drops, ending my words.

"No," Adrian whispers. "No."

Basil, in nothing but his boxers, whimpers at the sound of our voices. Aris, that sick motherfucker, did this to our friend. A friend who we wrongfully thought was a rat was nothing more than a victim. He's lying on the bed, his torso cut from throat to groin. His body has been pulled apart to expose his organs. I step closer and notice that he's been freshly packed with ice. Lots of it.

"He's here," I hiss.

"N-No," Basil croaks. "Gone."

Adrian jolts from his stupor and sits beside Basil on the bed. I mimic his actions, coming up on the other side. As Adrian grabs Basil's hand and lets out a choked sound, I drag my stare over his open torso. His intestines have been pulled out some and hang over the sides of his ribs, dripping in sticky blood. He has to be in agonizing pain.

"We need to call an ambulance," I mutter, fixated on the horrific sight.

Adrian jerks his head my way. "That shit isn't fixable, Boss." His cheeks are wet with tears. "I thought he was a rat."

I sit down next to Basil and frown at him. "We didn't think you were a rat," I explain. "We just figured you were with one. And we were right. Where's he headed next? Give me anything and I'll put you out of your misery."

Basil's face scrunches. "H-He wants b-back at the h-hotel…"

"Why?" I growl. "We've not even been there."

"Info…info…" He groans.

"Information?"

"Yesss," Basil whispers.

Aris is nothing without his numbers and he wants them back. Makes fucking sense. Over my dead body.

"You served me well," I tell Basil. "Say goodbye to Adrian."

Adrian makes a growling sound of a pained animal. He leans forward and presses his forehead to Basil's. "I love you, brother," Adrian tells Basil. He sighs hard and then he's gone, leaving me alone with Basil.

"Thank you," I mutter, pulling out my Glock. "A promise is a promise."

Holding the barrel against his temple, I stare into Basil's dark eyes so he doesn't have to die alone, and I pull the trigger.

Aris will pay for this.

His time is running out.

chapter
twenty-four

Talia

"How are you doing?" I ask Kostas. He's standing in front of the mirror, tying his tie, and looks like he's a million miles away. When he got home last night, he filled me in on everything. His private plane has been blown to bits, and Basil was found in a shitty motel, alone and dying.

I didn't know him well, but from what I've seen, Kostas, Adrian, and Basil were all close. As close to friends as three men in this world can be. The way he looked at me, with sad, distant eyes when he told me about his death, had me wanting to hold him close.

Kostas won't ever say it, but I think he blames himself for Basil's death. If he had looked harder, maybe he would've found him in time. My poor husband has suffered so much loss in his life, I don't know how he even gets out of bed in the morning. If I were knocked down as many times as him, I don't think I would be able to get up.

But in typical Kostas fashion, he quickly schooled his features and pretended like everything was okay. He made love to me slowly and told me no less than a dozen times he's going to catch his brother.

"I'm okay," he says for the millionth time, glancing at my reflection in the mirror. "How about I pick up dinner on my way home to make up for the one I fucked up the other night?"

He walks over and sits on the edge of the bed where Zoe and I are still lying. Zoe likes to wake up at the crack of dawn, have a bottle, and then come back to bed with Kostas and me for early morning snuggles. I warned Kostas the first time she did it, she would keep doing it. He just shrugged and said he hoped so.

"You already made up for that dinner." I smile, recalling the way he made up for it several times. First with his tongue, and then a couple more times with his cock.

Kostas smirks, knowing what's running through my head. "Still, I'll pick up dinner." He leans over and kisses my lips. Groaning into his mouth, I grab his lapels and try to pull him back into bed.

He chuckles and stands. "Not happening, *moró mou*. I have another appointment with the insurance adjuster."

"For the plane?"

"Yeah." He pecks my lips one more time. "I should be home early. Behave."

A little while later, Zoe wakes up drooling and cranky. I think another tooth is coming in. After she's changed and fed, I give her to my mom to hold so I can find one of the men to go to the store to pick up medicine.

As I'm opening the front door, I run straight into Fowler. Our bodies collide and his hands land on my hips. Not wanting him to touch me, I move out of his reach, but his fingers are digging into my skin, preventing me from moving.

"Let go of me," I hiss, swatting at his hands.

"Would you rather I let you fall?" He smirks evilly.

Anger burns through me and I'm seconds from clawing his face apart.

"Get your fucking hands off my sister," Phoenix growls, walking up behind Fowler. "Now."

Fowler stares me down in an arrogant way that leads me to believe he thinks he's powerful and untouchable. But based on the fury rippling from my brother and when Kostas gets wind of this, this asshole will learn his place in my home—in my world.

"My bad." He releases his hold on me and raises his palms into the air.

"Why the fuck were you touching her?" Phoenix accuses. "Didn't we already talk about this?" He steps into Fowler's face.

Fowler grins wide, as if they're two old friends in on a joke. "Bro, I didn't touch her—" Fowler begins, but Phoenix cuts him off.

"I'm *not* your bro."

Fowler just laughs. "Look, *man*, she ran into me and I caught her so she didn't bust her ass. Next time I'll just let her fall." He shrugs and walks around Phoenix.

"Two strikes," Phoenix calls over his shoulder.

He says it loud enough that Fowler can hear him, but he keeps walking, pretending he doesn't.

"That guy seriously rubs me the wrong way," I tell Phoenix.

"Yeah, he's a punk."

"What's with the two strikes?" I ask, curious.

"Three strikes and he's out." He looks over his shoulder then back at me. "Why were you coming out here?"

"Zoe is teething. I need someone to run to the store to buy her pain medicine."

"Is she okay?" Phoenix's brows furrow in concern. I never imagined I would ever have my brother in my life, let alone my daughter's. And I definitely never thought Phoenix would be such a hands-on uncle. Growing up, I only got to see him for a short time over the summer, or for the holidays when he would visit. I always assumed he was just like Niles—selfish and irresponsible. But he's actually nothing like him. His only fault was that he was loyal to his dad—until he wasn't.

"She's fine. I just want to make sure she's not in pain. She's whining and being cranky."

"Sounds a lot like her mom." Phoenix smirks.

"Hush it." I push his shoulder playfully.

"I'll send Fowler to go get it." He laughs. "He's not doing shit anyway, so he can play errand boy. Make himself useful."

"I think it's time for me to go home," Mom says. We're sitting on the floor in Zoe's nursery, watching as she crawls all over the place, knocking blocks over and smashing the keys to her soft play piano.

"Already?" I pout. I love having my mom here with me. Once she goes back to Italy, who knows when I will see her again.

"Already?" She laughs. "I've been here for a month."

My pout deepens, my bottom lip jutting out dramatically. "But I'm going to miss you, and so is Zoe."

"I know, *cara mia*, but Stefano isn't good at fending for

himself. He's complained every day that the cook isn't making what he likes." She rolls her eyes in mock annoyance. "Imagine if you were away from Kostas for a few days? Or a week?"

I laugh at the thought. Kostas would never let that happen. He'd be all growly and then demand he either goes with me or I don't go. "I get it. So how much longer do I get you?"

"Stefano found a flight for next week. So we have a little more time together." She gives me a soft smile.

"Okay, I'll take it."

Zoe stops banging on the piano and turns to me. Her eyes well up with tears and she shoves her tiny fist into her mouth. Fowler should be back by now with her medicine.

"I'm going to go see if Fowler is back with Zoe's medicine yet. Can you hold her?"

"Of course," Mom says, taking Zoe into her arms. "You know, when you and Phoenix were babies, we just rubbed whiskey on your gums."

I bark out a laugh. "I think we'll stick to good old Tylenol."

I run downstairs and spot one of the men on the phone in the kitchen. Not wanting to interrupt him, I head out the front door. The vehicle Fowler uses is parked in the driveway, so I go in search of him. I find him standing on the side of the house. I'm about to call out his name when I see he has his phone pressed up to his ear. Instead, I walk forward a few steps so I can listen.

"The plane is totaled," he says then stays quiet, listening to whoever is on the other line. I'm curious as to who he's speaking to since all of Kostas's men already know the plane is totaled.

"The bitch and the baby? That's going to cost you big

time. Last time I checked you don't have that kind of money. If you want me to grab them, I'm going to need to see the money first."

Oh my God! The bitch and the baby? There's only one bitch around here with a baby, and that's me. I consider sticking around to hear whatever else he's going to say, but decide I've heard enough to know this guy is bad fucking news. It's why he doesn't give a shit about anything Phoenix or Kostas threaten. He's not working for them… He's working for Aris. He's a damn rat!

Needing to get to my daughter and mom to make sure they're safe, I turn and run back into the house and up the stairs. The first thing I need is my gun. There's no way I'm chancing that asshole kidnapping Zoe and me and bringing us back to Aris.

Since my bedroom is before Zoe's, I pop in there to grab my gun from the nightstand. But as I'm grabbing it, I hear footsteps behind me, and a chill runs up my spine. Somehow Fowler knows I heard him.

Not chancing him either killing or kidnapping me, I quickly flip the safety off and turn around with the gun aimed directly at him. He has his aimed at me as well.

"Easy, girl," he starts, an evil glint in his eye as he steps forward.

Pop!

I choke on a gasp as the blood swells, blooming like a flower. Holy shit. His eyes widen as he grabs his side. He wasn't expecting me to be packing and he sure as hell didn't expect me to shoot. He should've, though. I'm married to the most powerful mob boss in the country. Of course he's going to make sure I can defend myself.

Pop!

I waste no time squeezing on the trigger again. This bullet goes through his arm and he drops the gun.

We both go after it at the same time, but as I'm diving down to grab it, Fowler drops to the ground. When I look up, I find Phoenix standing in the doorway with a gun in his hand.

"Thank you," I breathe. I glance over at Fowler and he's knocked out, the side of his head bleeding. Phoenix must've hit him with the butt of his gun.

"I'll always have your back, sis," he says, reaching his hand out to help me up.

"How did you know?" I ask, standing and handing him the gun.

"Overheard him talking on the phone. Saw you listening as well, but I didn't want to draw attention to you. As soon as you ran, he turned around, and I knew he saw you." He kicks Fowler in the stomach so he rolls over onto his back. He's bleeding heavily onto my carpet. Great, I'll probably never get that stain out.

"I'm so glad you're here." I run into Phoenix's arms.

"Eh, looks like you were handling yourself just fine." He kisses the top of my head.

"I need to go make sure Mom and Zoe are safe," I tell him. "I don't know who we can even trust. I'm going to have her lock herself in the room. Can you tie this fucker up and call Kostas?"

Phoenix's lips curl into a wide grin.

"What?" I ask, confused.

"Nothing." He shakes his head. "I just hope one day I find a woman like you. Kostas got himself a good one. He better treat you right."

"He more than treats me right," I tell him. "He treats me like his queen."

When I get to Zoe's room, the door is closed and locked. "Mom," I call out.

"Talia! I heard a gunshot! Are you okay?" she says through the door.

"Yes, I'm okay. You can open the door." I want to make sure nobody is in there. I knew something was up with Fowler. Who knows who else is a rat.

When she opens the door, I sigh in relief at the sight of my daughter bouncing up and down in her crib. "Go ahead and lock the door again. Phoenix has Fowler, and Kostas will be on his way shortly. Don't open the door unless it's one of us."

"Okay, be safe, sweetheart." She gives me a kiss on my cheek.

I get back to the room to find Phoenix has Fowler propped up in my reading chair and has used my robe belt to tie his hands. He's awake, but his head is hanging down. I bet he has a massive migraine. The thought makes me laugh. When my husband is done with him, a migraine will be the least of what he feels.

"What the fuck are you laughing at?" Fowler hisses. "You think tying me up is going to stop Aris from getting to you again?" He laughs wickedly, and I take a step back. Gone is the pervy flirt, and present is a ruthless mobster. "That man is on a revenge mission, and he ain't gonna stop until he has everything Kostas cares about. Mark my fucking words."

The room chills several degrees like a cold storm has surged into our bedroom, ready to destroy everything in its path.

"My brother will get to my wife again over my dead fucking body," Kostas says, entering the room. He saunters over to Fowler like he doesn't have a care in the world. But I can see the darkness in his usually light eyes. He's pissed and he's going to make Fowler pay…after he makes him talk.

"We can make this easy or difficult. Are you going to tell me where my brother is, or am I going to beat it out of you?" Kostas cracks his neck to one side and then to the other, the bones popping in an intimidating way.

Fowler laughs. "I'm not saying shit." He spits at Kostas. "I already know my death warrant's been signed. I'm not going down a fucking rat."

Kostas glowers at him as he sheds his jacket and rolls up his sleeves. "The hard way it is." He turns to me, and I give a look that tells him I'm not going anywhere. I'll be damned if I don't get to see this asshole get what's coming to him. Kostas simply shakes his head, not even bothering to argue.

Kostas unbuckles his belt and pulls it through the loops. For a second, I wonder if he's going to whip Fowler with his belt, but instead he wraps it around his neck, tightening it so tight, Fowler's veins in his neck and face bulge. He doesn't stop until Fowler's face is bright red.

"This is for teaming with the wrong side." He tightens it some more, and I worry he's going to kill him before he gets any information out of him.

"And this is for even *thinking* you would try to take my daughter and wife from me." Kostas tightens the belt, and Fowler's survival instincts kick in. He tries to wriggle his body to get free. His head lashes back and forth as his face color turns to a deep crimson.

"Sis, you sure you wanna be here for this?" Phoenix asks, his tone laced with worry.

"She's not going anywhere," Kostas says, answering for me. "Your sweet little sister has quite the dark side in her." While still choking Fowler, he looks back and shoots me a knowing smirk, causing my belly to flutter with butterflies. Jesus, I think I might be as crazy as my husband.

chapter
twenty-five

Kostas

WHEN I'D GOTTEN THE TEXT FROM PHOENIX, I'D seen red. But thankfully, Talia's brother is one of the few people I can trust around here. He'd been onto Fowler's bullshit already and had his eye on him. And when the fucker thought he could hurt *my fucking wife*, she shot him.

Good girl.

Good goddamn girl.

The prick is whining and hissing against the leather belt that has him in a chokehold, but all I can do is admire my wife. She looks borderline angelic in her yellow sundress and sunny hair that hangs down her back in what she calls beach waves. Even the smile on her plump red lips is serene. It's the eyes, though.

Brilliant and blazing.

Wickedly blue.

A monster who teases my own.

If I didn't have this dickhead to torture, I'd bend her over my bed right now and take her bloody cunt. I'd smack her ass in the way bad girls get their reward and use my crimson-soaked dick to push between her cheeks, taking her where she doesn't bleed but sure as fuck will feel like it.

Having a hard-on with a rat in my presence is inconvenient.

"Take him to the garage. This shit is going to get bloody." I nod at Phoenix. "Don't kill him yet."

While Phoenix handles him, I grab Talia's wrist and haul her into our giant closet. I close the door and then pounce on her. My lips crash to hers as I grab her ass.

"I was fucking terrified something happened to you," I growl, nipping at her bottom lip. "And here you are, ruling over your mere mortals like the queen you are. You make me proud, *zoí mou.*"

She kisses me hard and works at my tie. "You can't wear your good tie to cut off limbs, husband."

"And sundresses are meant for the beach, not stabbing rats," I tell her, ripping at the fabric and pulling it down one shoulder so I can kiss her bare skin. "As much as I want to fuck my gorgeous wife, I need to get down there and find answers."

She grumbles as she grips my dick through my slacks. "You can't go down there with this." She squeezes me. "You'll accidentally poke someone's eye out." When she drops to her knees, I groan in pleasure. Her wicked grin is back as she tugs at my zipper and reaches into my boxers to free my cock. She pulls it through the zipper hole and admires it with exaggerated excitement.

Little brat.

Playful and sexy in a time where we need to be ruthless and evil...and yet I want to make them wait for five goddamn minutes so my wife can suck my dick.

Her pink tongue darts out, wetting my tip, and she circles it in a teasing way. I grip a handful of her blond hair and pin her with a fierce stare.

"Wrap your fat lips around my dick," I growl.

She scowls. "Fat?"

Oh, Jesus, fuck.

"Plump. Juicy. Perfect. Your lips were made for sucking dick, Talia. Fucking own it."

This earns me a smile and then she wraps those lovely lips around my thick, veiny cock, ravishing me with her hot mouth. I grunt and flex my hips, slightly fucking her mouth. Her teeth scrape along my flesh and her blue eyes dart up to mine, a warning gleaming in them. I take her challenge and buck again. She gags and purposefully drags her teeth up my shaft to the crown. Her cheeks indent as she sucks on the crown, hard and unyielding, as though she can bleed me dry of cum with such a simple maneuver. It nearly fucking works. A growl rumbles through me and I thrust again. Her throat constricts when my tip slides into its tight, warm depths.

She's so fucking pretty when her blue eyes water when she tries to swallow me whole.

"I'm going to come down your throat and then tonight I'm going to come in your ass," I tell her smugly, daring her to challenge me.

She doesn't because it's hard to argue with a nine-inch dick for a lollipop down your throat. Her slender fingers massage my balls before she twists slightly, reminding me of the fact that just because she's on her knees, it means nothing.

She. Fucking. Owns. Me.

Seeing her so goddamn powerful on her knees with

a monster's balls in her grip has me snarling with my release. She takes me deeper in her throat the moment that first burst of cum hits her throat. I hiss as my dick is swallowed down her needy throat. I flex my ass cheeks as I milk the rest of my cum into her hot mouth and then I pull away abruptly.

Talia rises to her feet and kisses my lips as she tucks my wet cock back into my slacks.

"Good boy," she purrs. "Now let's go torture that motherfucker."

It's true love with this one.

Talia leans against the wall, quietly watching, while Phoenix paces the floor in front of Fowler. Adrian has Fowler's phone and is already tracing numbers to locations. He'll work his tech side to get information while Phoenix and I do it the good old-fashioned way: by brute force.

Fowler's shirt has been removed and someone poured superglue in his gunshot wounds to keep him from bleeding out. That shit has to hurt like a bitch. Exactly what we wanted, too. It's only going to get worse from here.

"Where's Aris?" I ask coolly, fiddling with the tip of my knife.

He spits at Phoenix's feet. "Fuck you."

Phoenix bitch slaps him, making Fowler cry out in surprise. These men can take punches, but a slap to the face like a fucking girl is jarring to them. He gapes at Phoenix incredulously.

"You tell me where my brother is and we'll let you live."

I snort. "Man, I can't even say that with a straight face. How about this? We'll let you die quicker if you tell us where he is."

"I won't tell you shit," Fowler snaps.

"So you don't need your tongue then?" I step forward, loving the way his eyes widen marginally so.

"He didn't get a chance to tell me before your cunt wife—" Fowler starts.

Phoenix bitch slaps him again and snarls at him. "Her name is Talia. Use her name."

Fowler is pissed, but he rethinks his fight because he grits out his words. "Talia interrupted."

"Give us something," I say calmly. "Anything."

"What will you give me?" Fowler attempts to negotiate. "Maybe I'll tell you what I know, but I need something in return."

"You give me the information and I will cut you loose." I smirk at him. "Trust me?"

"I *don't* trust you, though," he says, scowling.

"You don't have many options," Talia reminds him.

Fowler snaps his head her way and glowers at her, but not before raking his eyes boldly down her body. This fucker has a death wish. He thinks he has the upper hand. That if he'll be openly salacious against her, I'll just end him now and put him out of this misery. When he licks his lips suggestively, I consider it, but Phoenix bitch slaps the look right off his face.

"What the fuck man?" Fowler bellows. "Stop fucking slapping me."

Phoenix smirks at me. "This is the most fun I've had… ever, frankly. Every time you open your bitch-ass mouth to spew more bullshit, I'm gonna slap the words right out of it.

Man the fuck up, Fowler. Tell us what you know and you'll die like you have a pair of balls between those legs."

"Agia Fotia. There's a hotel there that the Galanis used to hide out in. You know it?" Fowler asks.

I give him a clipped nod and then cut my eyes over to Talia. She slips from the room, hopefully to pass on the news to Adrian.

"Yeah, I know it. Is he there?" I demand, stepping closer.

"Fuck if I know, but he mentioned a hotel there in our last conversation. Didn't say if he was going there or not because your cunt—"

I press my blade to his lips, glaring down at him. "Careful, rat. We're not done talking and if you keep calling my wife a cunt, I'm going to cut your tongue from your throat. I'll make you learn goddamn sign language to finish this conversation. Don't fucking test me."

Blood trickles down his chin and I pull the blade away.

"We never got to finish our conversation," he gripes, before licking the new cut on his bottom lip.

Talia returns and gives me a nod before mouthing, "Adrian," to me. At least he can be checking our contacts there before this dick sends us on a wild goose chase.

"What's he planning next?" I ask.

"I don't fucking know." Fowler glowers at me.

"What do you know?"

"Nothing else."

Well, I guess our time here is over.

"Look at my wife," I order.

Now the greasy motherfucker tries to disobey me. Phoenix steps behind him and grabs his hair, yanking his head to the side.

"Boss says look," Phoenix growls, "you fucking look."

"And when Boss says keep your eyes to yourself, you keep them to your fucking self." I whistle for Talia. "Come here, woman, and hold my knife."

I sense her hesitation, but she won't undermine me now. She walks over to us and takes the knife from me. Fowler watches her with pure hatred that burns hot through my veins. He thinks I'm going to make her cut him or stab him. She's not fucking touching him.

"Like what you see?" I purr, my voice deceptively calm.

"Looks like a spoiled, used cunt—AHHH!"

I dig my thumbs into his eyes hard, cutting past the inner membrane inside his lower eyelids. His screams are otherworldly as he thrashes in his chair. Phoenix holds him in place as I rip through the flesh beneath his eyeballs. Vomit spews out at me when I pull my thumbs away and blood gushes down his cheeks. I flip my palms up and push three fingers into each hole beneath his eyeballs before curling them up around the back side of his eyeballs. He sputters and gurgles and hisses. With a hard yank, I relieve him of his wandering eyes, leaving two bloody, gaping holes in his head.

Talia has retreated, her back now against the wall. Good. I want her away from this sick fuck. I open my palms to look at the rat's eyes. Beady and fucking useless now. I toss them on the ground and Phoenix stomps them with his combat boot. Fowler has officially been renamed Howler because he's crying out like he's a fucking wolf lost from his pack.

Adrian enters the garage and his dark eyes gleam with approval. He hates this fucker too. When he nods at me, I know the intel is good. We'll need to leave soon.

"Toss me the knife," I say to my wife.

She throws it at me and it clatters at my feet. I pick it up and then begin sawing Howler free. He squawks and carries on like the little bitch he is.

"What now?" Phoenix asks, violence gleaming in his eyes that match Talia's.

"A promise is a promise," I reply, shrugging. "I told the fucker I'd cut him loose if he gave us information." Then, I grin at Phoenix. "But you, man, you didn't promise him a damn thing. He's all yours. I need you here protecting Melody and Zoe. Talia and I are going on a second honeymoon."

After we showered, changed, and packed some weapons, Talia and I headed out to Agia Fotia Beach with Adrian following behind in his new Jeep. Fucking Phoenix corrupted him with that corny-ass Jeep shit. But, since my wife smashed Adrian's car, it was only fair I bought him a new toy. Even if the toy is meant for a man twenty years his junior.

To an outsider, Talia and I in my Maserati look like any other rich couple. Carefree and happy. We're happy, that's for damn sure. And we'll be carefree the moment I have my hands around my brother's throat. Until then, we'll keep hunting his awful ass down.

"We're almost there," she says, yawning. "Are we really going to stay at the beach house?"

"You mean the Cliffside monster stairs home?"

She laughs. "Remember when I made you carry me up all those steps?"

"Remember when I fucked you on four hundred rocks and made you mine?"

We both smile.

"It won't always be like this," I promise her. "The people in Greece know they can't fuck with me. They can try and I'll hunt their asses down. If they're smart, they'll pay their taxes, do my bidding, and be fucking merry."

"Is that all?" she asks dryly. "Want them to suck your dick too?"

"That's your job," I tell her with a smirk.

"You have to admit, you like it when I negotiate using blowjobs."

"Your blowjobs are the true secret behind world peace. Too bad you only give them to a tyrant."

She taps at her lips and feigns a thoughtful look. "Maybe I should spread the love around."

"Maybe I should spread you over my lap and make you fuck me the rest of the way."

"I did not come through all this to die in a ditch because my sex freak husband wanted to have more period sex while driving a million-dollar car."

Three mil, but who's counting.

"There's always the ride home," I tease, gripping her jean-clad thigh.

The rest of the trip we drive in contented silence. I know she's nervous about finding him, but I'm eager as hell. It's long overdue.

Rather than going to the hotel the Galanis always stayed at, I take her straight to the Cliffside home. It's my first destination. We pull into the driveway and I lean over to kiss Talia.

"How long will it take to find out if Aris is at the hotel?" she asks once we park.

"He's not there," I state as I climb out of the car.

She follows me, grabbing my hand. "What? What do you mean?"

"If there's one thing I know about my brother, it's that he likes to play games. He doesn't trust anyone. You think he'd give such an obvious clue to his man?"

Talia stops to frown at me. "No."

I caress her cheek. "No, because if the man was found out, then he'd tell me. And if Aris knows me, he had to know I'd find out because I'm not fucking stupid."

Her plump lips purse, making my dick thicken with need. Not now, but soon, I'll have those lips on me again. "He wanted to lure you to the hotel." She lets out a rush of relieved breath. "So we outsmarted him then?"

"Did we?" I muse aloud, darting my eyes to the house.

Her blue eyes flicker with fear, but I shush her with a kiss. "He knew we'd stay here if we came looking for him at that hotel. He'd attempt to catch us off guard."

She pulls away, whirling around. "Where's Adrian?"

"Don't worry about that," I say with a grin as I lead her over to the front door. "Let's get you inside. I want to fuck you in the hot tub."

Her shoulders are tense, but she trusts me as I guide her into the home. As soon as we walk inside, we see Aris. Gun in hand and evil fucking smile on his face.

And then Adrian tackles him from behind.

Aris's eyes blink open slowly. He looks like shit. I'm not sure he's showered recently and the scruffy beard he's sporting doesn't make him look refined. It makes him look like trash.

That's what he is to me.

Trash.

Ready to be kicked to the goddamn curb. Indefinitely.

"The almighty Demetriou reigns," Aris snarls, finding his venom past the haze of recently being knocked out.

I snort. "Nothing's changed, little brother."

His brown eyes dart to Talia, who's perched in my lap like a fucking goddess waiting to be worshiped. Rather than worshiping his queen, he spits her way. She flinches and I hate that he holds some sort of power over her.

Not for long.

Adrian is still as a statue, leaned against the wall like a fucking gargoyle. All it takes is Aris to move the wrong way and Adrian will pounce on him, gutting him like he gutted Basil. The violence ripples from Adrian in waves like heat from the sun. Powerful, malevolent, unforgiving.

"You didn't think you'd go on terrorizing me and not get caught in my web eventually, did you?" I stroke my fingers through Talia's blond hair, my eyes fixed on him. "You're caught now. Nothing but a useless fucking moth, struggling to get free." I flash him a smug grin. "You, Aris fucking Demetriou, are a victim now. Something to be destroyed and ruined. Forgotten."

"Fuck you," he snarls. "Your theatrics are boring, Kostas. Get the hell on with it."

"Personally," Talia pipes up, her voice wavering slightly. "I find his *theatrics* quite charming."

"You always were a dumb bitch," Aris growls, fighting against his restraints.

"They're mouthy as fuck when they're looking death in the eye," Adrian bellows from across the room, making the three of us look his way. His hateful glare is fixated on Aris. I should let him deal with my brother, but that wouldn't be fair to Talia. She suffered too. This is her vengeance.

"I've been planning your death for a while now," I tell Aris. "I imagined all the ways I'd cut you and drain you of your blood. How I'd make you suffer slowly. But then I realized it's not up to me." I pat Talia's thigh. "It's up to her."

She rises from my lap and I rake my eyes down her perfect jean-clad ass.

"I trusted you," she says, her voice small as she picks up the knife from the table. "I tried to comfort you."

"Aww," Aris taunts, his nostrils flaring. "You thought your magical pussy would make me all better? Sorry, princess, but your cunt is just like every other cunt out there. Although, you squealed like a little pig when I shoved my dick in it."

She freezes and I'm tempted to leap over the table to crush his fucking skull. But I won't. Not unless she asks me to. And my brave wife doesn't ask for help. She slowly approaches him, like a viper ready to strike. The knife in her grip gleams in the light.

"You raped me," she accuses, her voice breaking. "You took advantage of my kindness and then you took advantage of me."

He laughs hatefully. "It didn't feel like rape when you were impaled on my cock. It felt like vindication." He sneers at me. "How does it feel knowing I popped that cherry, big brother? Does it burn you up every night knowing your brother's dick has been inside your wife? Does it—what the fuck?"

Blood runs down his cheek from the slash of the knife. Her body trembles as she stares down at him.

"It was rape and you know it," she seethes. "Admit it and I'll let you keep your cock."

"My cock belongs to you, though, bitch," he taunts. "You

damn near begged for it the whole time I had you holed away from Kostas. If Selene weren't there, you know we would've already made another baby."

She slashes again, this time ripping through his bottom lip. Blood runs thick down his chin. His eyes turn wild as he realizes he's dying in this living room. Tonight. At the hand of the one he brutalized.

Eye for a fucking eye.

Even Howler learned that lesson.

"Say it," she orders. "Say it or I'll cut you a thousand times. Don't fucking test me, Aris. I will. I'll cut you for every time I lied to your face and told you Zoe was your daughter."

His nostrils flare. "I raped you because I could," he sneers. "I haven't deflowered a virgin since I was a fucking teenager. I should have taken your ass instead."

She turns her head to look at me, tears gleaming in her blue eyes. Even had he not admitted, I knew the truth. But this was something she clearly needed to hear. To confirm. For me to know without a shadow of a doubt. This is her vengeance, not mine.

Yes, he took and took from me, but he didn't take that.

He stole her virginity and her freedom. He stole her happiness.

For that, she will make him pay.

I give her a nod of support and a wink.

"You thought you could bring down my husband, but you couldn't," she whispers, turning back to him. "You couldn't because you were always the weak one. The un-loved one. The least favorite. Poor little Aris. Only Mommy loved you, but even still, she loved you equal to your brother."

"Fuck you," he roars. "Don't ever talk about my mother."

"Your mother is rolling in her grave because the man she hated most is the man you turned out to be," Talia continues, her body vibrating with power. "You turned into him. Ezio. You're that spineless bastard, weak and afraid."

"I am not like that motherfucker!" he screams, his face turning purple with rage.

Aww, someone still has daddy issues.

"You always did look more like the gardener," I muse aloud.

Talia laughs. "How does it feel to be powerless? You only had the illusion of power for a short while there. Your brother always wielded it and it drove you fucking crazy. He got the empire, he got the girl, and he got the kid." She slashes again, this time slicing a big gash on the side of his neck. "What do you have, Aris? A mediocre cock in your pants and a burning desire to be him?" She points her knife at me. "Well, you're not him. Not even close."

"Go to hell," Aris slurs, his skin quickly paling with the blood loss that's pouring like rivers down the side of his neck.

She straddles his thighs and presses the tip of the blade against his chest, right over his heart. "You soon will." Her body trembles, but she doesn't make the move.

"Talia?" I ask, rising to my feet.

A sob chokes her. "I want to, but…"

Walking over to her, I stare down at my brother she's singlehandedly ruined with her knife. I could end him right now. Hell, we could leave him and he'd bleed to death within minutes. That won't bring her peace, though. She needs to do this.

I lean forward and wrap my arms around her. My hand grips hers on the hilt of the knife. Nuzzling her hair with my nose, I inhale her sweet and sweaty scent. I kiss her hair and murmur my words against her head.

"Ready, *zoí mou*?"

"Yes," she breathes.

I use my other hand to cover the top of the hilt of the knife and drive it forward. Her hand flexes beneath mine, but she doesn't squirm away. Together, we push the blade past his flesh and into his chest. Together, we pierce his heart. Together, we breathe raggedly as we watch the life quietly drain from the monster in our lives.

Releasing the knife, I hook my arms around her middle and pull her away from him. I walk her outside so Adrian can deal with the body. She turns in my arms, sobbing against my chest. I stroke her hair and kiss her head. The waves crash down below.

"It's over now, *moró mou*. You can be happy."

She pulls away and places her blood-splattered hands on my cheeks. Her blue eyes are watery as she regards me. "I am happy, Kostas. With you, never doubt that."

"I love you," I murmur. "My beautiful, brave, fiery wife."

"I love you more."

"Impossible," I growl, nipping at her juicy lip.

A smile tugs at her lips. "Then prove it."

"Anything."

"Give me a piggyback down to the beach."

All those stairs. All. Those. Fucking Stairs.

"Aww, I'm only teasing," she says, laughing. "You should have seen your face!"

With a growl, I scoop her into my arms.

I carry her down all those goddamn stairs. Every last

one of them. And when I've fucked her in the warm sea and made her scream my name in pleasure, I'll carry her back up all those motherfucking steps. Every grueling one.

I'll carry her anywhere.

To the ends of the earth. Through heaven and hell. And into the next life.

She's fucking mine forever.

epilogue

Talia
One Year Later

"Mommy, what's this?" Zoe asks, pointing at the exquisite fountain in the middle of the courtyard.

With me almost two weeks overdue, we decided to drive over to the Pérasma Hotel with Kostas today to hang out, swim a little, and get some sun while being waited on.

When Zoe asked if we could go for a walk, I figured it would be the perfect opportunity to try to walk my over-ly-pregnant behind into labor. Big mistake. Because now I've plopped myself onto the wicker lounge chair to relax for a minute, and there's a good possibility I may never get back up.

Not wanting to tell her what she's pointing to is Bernini's *Rape of Proserpina*, I go with a more childproof answer. "It's a statue of a man and a woman."

"Not just any man and woman," a masculine voice says, catching my attention. I glance over and spot my sexy husband sauntering over. Unlike the first time I saw him in this very spot, dressed casual in khakis and a button-down shirt, today he's sporting his power suit. I would take him either way, but truth be told, my favorite Kostas is the one without any clothes on in our bed.

Kostas picks Zoe up and she squeals in excitement. "This statue is of Pluto and Proserpina," he tells her as if she can understand. He always talks to her like she's an adult. It's oddly adorable.

"Pluto?" she questions. "Like the doggy?"

He gives me a confused look.

"Pluto is the cute puppy on Disney," I explain.

He laughs and shakes his head. "No, this Pluto was a very powerful god." He gives me a knowing look. "He stole Proserpina and brought her into the Underworld. And because he loved her so much, he tricked her into staying by tempting her with delicious food. She, of course, took the bait and was sentenced to remain with him for the rest of eternity."

I grin at his version of the story. It was my version. The safe version. The one that made Pluto out to be the bad guy and kept Proserpina innocent. But as I look at my handsome husband holding our daughter in his arms, I realize my view of the story has changed. That I've changed.

"He didn't trick her," I say out loud.

Kostas's eyes gleam with excitement. "No?"

"No, that would be giving him too much credit and her not enough," I admit. "I think you were right before. If she didn't want to stay, she wouldn't have eaten the seeds. But she did so because she wanted to."

I attempt to stand, but my big belly weighs me down.

"*Moró mou*," Kostas says. "Let me help you." He sets Zoe down, who runs over to the fountain to dip her hand in the water.

As he helps pull me into a standing position, my stomach tightens, and I cringe slightly at the pain that shoots down my back. "I made Proserpina out to be the damsel in distress," I tell him. "The victim, but maybe she wasn't. Maybe she was just scared and he helped her come to the realization of what she already knew."

"And what's that?" Kostas asks, gripping the curve of my hips and leaning over to kiss my lips.

"That she was always meant to be loved by Pluto and to be the Queen of the Underworld."

I can imagine how she felt. When she met Pluto, there was no turning back. She fell for him the moment she laid eyes on him. He didn't have to drag her there, because she belonged there. She just needed to come home.

Another pain shoots down my back and then it feels as though I've peed myself. I glance down and liquid is dripping down my legs under my bathing suit.

"Talia, are you okay?" Kostas asks, his eyes widening in fear. It's not often I see my husband appear to be scared.

"Yeah." I nod with a smile. "But our baby is finally coming."

Kostas

Fuck. Fuck. Fuck.

Fuck. Fuck. Fuck.

Fuck. Fuck. Fuck.

"Stop saying fuck," Talia seethes, "or I will rip your tongue out of your mouth."

The doctor smirks at me from between her legs and I tense. Clearly I've been chanting the words that have been running inside my head from the moment she was put into this hospital bed. I wonder if she heard the other ones.

She's brave and resilient and strong.

The best mother in the world.

Beautiful beyond reason.

"A real Casanova, that one," the nurse says to Talia, winking.

I look down to find Talia's eyes watering. "I love you," she whimpers.

Leaning down, I kiss her plump lips. "I love you too. You're doing great."

"Oh shit," she whines. "I can't do this."

"You've done it before," I remind her.

"And her head wasn't as big as Nora's either!"

I can't help but grin at her. The moment we found out we were having another little girl, Talia asked if we could name her after my mother. It broke my heart and healed it all at once. Of course I said yes. My mother would be so fucking proud of me. She would've loved those girls with everything she had. Thankfully, we have Melody and she does the job of two grandmas at once.

"I see dark hair," the doctor says, his eyes crinkling with delight. "The baby is coming. Want to watch?"

I dart my eyes to Talia, who nods. I missed Zoe's birth, so seeing Nora's is a gift. Releasing Talia's hand, I shuffle down to the end of the bed.

"Holy shit," I utter, completely transfixed to see the head of my daughter trying to come through the small hole. "Talia, she's almost here."

"Another contraction," the nurse says. "That's it, honey, push and hold."

Talia bears down and the head begins to push out. When she can't push anymore, the dark hair disappears some. Another contraction hits right after the other and my incredible wife pushes harder. I'm awestruck by how strong she is—scrunched face in determination, purple flesh as she uses every ounce of strength she can muster, sweaty hair stuck to her forehead.

"There we go," the doctor says, drawing my attention back to our daughter.

Fuck. Fuck. Fuck.

Fuck. Fuck. Fuck.

"STOP SAYING FUCK!" Talia warns through gritted teeth.

I gape in part horror, part fascination as I stare at the head sticking out of my wife's body. A film of something covers her face and she's as purple as her mother. Birthing a baby is a fucking miraculous thing.

I gently caress Talia's thigh. "I can see her head, *moró mou*. She's so perfect."

Talia sobs but then she's pushing again. And again. And again. Until the baby seems to slide out of her body and into the doctor's waiting arms. Bloody and messy. Screaming at the top of her little lungs.

"Big baby girl," the doctor praises as he shuffles the squirming infant onto Talia's stomach. Blood is everywhere. The good kind of blood. The blood of miracles.

Talia's whole body trembles as she cries and admires our daughter.

"Want to cut the cord?"

I snap my eyes over to the doctor, who offers me a pair of scissors. Sure enough, the thick umbilical cord that's attached to our daughter needs removing. Will it hurt if I cut it? Can Talia feel it?

"Cut the cord, Kostas," Talia urges, her words no longer laced with violence. They're gentle and sweet and encouraging.

Frowning at the doctor, I shakily accept the scissors. "Are they going to feel it?"

"No, son, they're not going to feel it," he says, chuckling.

I've cut off limbs and eyeballs and every other body part imaginable.

So why the fuck do I feel like I'm going to pass out?

It's a cord. A tiny passage of nutrients our daughter no longer needs.

With bile rising in my throat and sweat coating my flesh, I start to snip through the cord. But it doesn't cut smooth and easy. I have to hack through the thick rope.

Fuck. Fuck. Fuck.

Fuck. Fuck. Fuck.

This time, Talia laughs.

"Baby ears are listening," she teases.

I manage to sever the cord, making Nora officially ours to take care of and protect. The weight of the responsibility nearly crushes me. But I've managed to do it with Talia and Zoe. What's one more?

As they continue to deliver the placenta, I abandon the scissors and opt not to watch that part. I may be a fucked-up mobster who's seen some shit, but I haven't seen that, nor do I fucking plan on it. No, I'd rather keep my eyes glued to our perfect daughter and her adoring mother.

"Zoe is going to be so proud," Talia tells me tearfully. "You think she's giving Uncle Fee hell?"

I snort. I hope so. Phoenix is a pussy-magnet player who's corrupted Adrian with his manwhore ways. When they're not working, they tear up the fucking town looking for women. I'm glad one little girl owns his heart. Now he'll have another one soon wrapped around his finger.

"I hope she tells him the names of all her stuffed animals," I say with a chuckle.

She has tons. Too many. Talia and I both have been the victims of her lengthy sessions of telling us the name of each and every one of them. If you interrupt, she starts over. If she forgets a name, she starts over. I've tortured many a men, but Zoe has invented a form of torture all on her own.

I'd say she got it from me, but that has Talia written all over it.

We admire her until they take her away to clean her up a bit and run some tests. Then, they hand our daughter back, bundled in a warm blanket.

"Want to hold her?" Talia asks, her smile serene.

I nod as I pick up the tiny thing. She weighs nothing. So light and fragile. As I pull her to my chest and cradle her, my eyes burn with emotion. I'll protect this little one like I do her sister and her mother. With everything I own until the day I die.

Nora scrunches her face and makes a crabby whining cry that has me chuckling. She's so damn cute. When I glance over at Talia, her bottom lip wobbles as tears streak down her cheeks.

"What's wrong?" I demand, alarmed at her crying.

She shakes her head. "Nothing, Kostas. Everything is right. Better than right. It's perfect."

I let out a relieved sigh and kiss my daughter's forehead. "I love you, *prinkípissa.*" *Princess.*

"You're a good man," Talia mutters, reaching her hand out for me.

Taking it, I give it a squeeze. "Only for you."

Our eyes lock and a million emotions pass between us.

Talia and I are the earth, the sun, the stars, and everything in between. We're evil and good, wrapped in one complicated ball of love. She challenges me. I provoke her. Vases get broken and words get said. Sometimes we fight like hellions straight from the bowels of the Underworld.

But we love hardest of all.

Fully. Passionately. Dangerously.

Our love is violent and messy, destructive for those who dare near it. It slaughters and slays. Powerful and intimidating to those around it. Love between a Demetriou king and queen is chaotic like the tropical storms that often ravish our seaside properties. We're a pull of two forces of nature, only working when orbiting the other.

Fate drew us together—victims of a complicated history of our parents.

Love kept us there.

"What are you thinking about?" Talia asks, her blue eyes gleaming with adoration and utter loyalty.

"You. Always you."

The End

****If you loved this duet, you'll love **Heath** also by K Webster and Nikki Ash!****

authornikkiash.com/co-written-books-by-k-webster-and-nikki-ash/

playlist

Head Above Water by Avril Lavigne

Complicated by Avril Lavigne

I'm a Mess by Bebe Rexha

Broken-hearted Girl by Beyoncé

Reason to Stay by Brett Young

Never be the Same by Camila Cabello

Consequences by Camila Cabello

The Scientist by Coldplay

Let it Go by James Bay

In Case by Demi Lovato

i hate u, i love u by Gnash

Desire by Meg Myers

Stay by Rihanna

Back to You by Louis Tomlinson

Bad Things by Machine Gun Kelly and Camila Cabello

Love on the Brain by Rihanna

Rock Bottom by Hailee Steinfeld

The Monster by Eminem

So Good by Zara Larsson

Remind Me to Forget by Kygo & Miguel

Him & I by G-Eazy & Halsey

Bad Blood by Taylor Swift

Mad by Ne-Yo

I'm a Mess by Ed Sheeran

acknowledgements from
K WEBSTER

Thank you to my husband! Love you, honey!

Nikki Ash, thank you for creating magic yet again with me! I always have so much fun writing with you!! These characters hold a special place in my heart…right next to you!

A huge thank you to my Krazy for K Webster's Books reader group. You all are insanely supportive and I can't thank you enough.

A gigantic thank you to those who always help me out. Elizabeth Clinton, Ella Stewart, Misty Walker, Holly Sparks, Jillian Ruize, Gina Behrends, Rosa Saucedo, Ker Dukey, and Nikki Ash—you ladies are my rock!

Thank you so much to Misty Walker for being the best friend a girl could ask for! Love you!!

Thank you so much, Wendy Rinebold, for proofing this book! You're a star, lady!!

A big thank you to my author friends who have given me your friendship and your support. You have no idea how much that means to me.

Thank you to all of my blogger friends both big and small

that go above and beyond to always share my stuff. You all rock! #AllBlogsMatter

Emily A. Lawrence, thank you SO much for editing this book. You rock!!

Thank you, Stacey Blake, for being amazing as always when formatting my books and in general. I love you! I love you! I love you!

Lastly but certainly not least of all, thank you to all of the wonderful readers out there who are willing to hear my story and enjoy my characters like I do. It means the world to me!

acknowledgements from
NIKKI ASH

hank you to my children. Your love and support is everything. To Bret, thank you for being the peanut butter to my jelly. Kristi Webster, thank you for believing in me and in this story. You make me a better person and a better writer. Thank you for your friendship. Nikki Ash's Fight Club reader group. In this crazy world, you guys are my safe place. Thank you! Thank you to all of the ladies who have my back. Stacy Garcia, Ashley Cormier, Brittany Ridge, Andrea Hebda, Tabitha Willbanks, Shannon Voyles, Kaylee Ryan, Lisa McKay, and Kristi Webster. I can't imagine doing any of this without you. Emily A. Lawrence, thank you for editing this book. Stacy Blake, thank you for making the book so pretty! Ena and Amanda with Enticing Journey, thank you for keeping me sane! I don't know what I would do without you guys! To all of the bloggers who take time out of their day to share their love of books, thank you for everything you do. And a huge thank you to the readers. There are so many books out there for you to read. Thank you for opening your hearts and allowing my words to speak to you. It's because of you, I get to continue to do what I love.

about
K WEBSTER

K Webster is a *USA Today* Bestselling author. Her titles have claimed many bestseller tags in numerous categories, are translated in multiple languages, and have been adapted into audiobooks. She lives in "Tornado Alley" with her husband, two children, and her baby dog named Blue. When she's not writing, she's reading, drinking copious amounts of coffee, and researching aliens.

Keep up with K Webster
Facebook: www.facebook.com/authorkwebster
Blog: authorkwebster.wordpress.com
Twitter: twitter.com/KristiWebster
Email: kristi@authorkwebster.com
Goodreads: www.goodreads.com/user/show/10439773-k-webster
Instagram: instagram.com/kristiwebster

about
NIKKI ASH

Nikki Ash resides in South Florida where she is an English teacher by day and a writer by night. When she's not writing, you can find her with a book in her hand. From the Boxcar Children, to Wuthering Heights, to the latest single parent romance, she has lived and breathed every type of book. While reading and writing are her passions, her two children are her entire world. You can probably find them at a Disney park before you would find them at home on the weekends!

Reading is like breathing in, writing is like breathing out.–
Pam Allyn

Contact Nikki Ash

Facebook: facebook.com/authornikkiash
Twitter: twitter.com/authornikkiash
Instagram: instagram.com/authornikkiash
Amazon: amazon.com/author/nikkiash
Website: www.authornikkiash.com

Nikki Ash's reader group:
www.facebook.com/groups/booksbynikkiash

Subscribe to Nikki Ash's newsletter:
bit.ly/NikkiAshNewsletter

books by
K WEBSTER

Taboo Treats:
Bad Bad Bad
Coach Long
Ex-Rated Attraction
Mr. Blakely
Easton
Crybaby
Lawn Boys
Malfeasance
Renner's Rules
The Glue
Dane
Enzo
Red Hot Winter
Dr. Dan

KKinky Reads Collection:
Share Me
Choke Me
Daddy Me
Watch Me
Hurt Me

Contemporary Romance Standalones:
Wicked Lies Boys Tell
Conheartists
The Day She Cried
Untimely You
Heath
Sundays are for Hangovers
A Merry Christmas with Judy
Zeke's Eden

Pretty Little Dolls Series:
Pretty Stolen Dolls (Book 1)
Pretty Lost Dolls (Book 2)
Pretty New Doll (Book 3)
Pretty Broken Dolls (Book 4)

The V Games Series:
Vlad (Book 1)
Ven (Book 2)
Vas (Book 3)

Four Fathers Books:
Pearson

Four Sons Books:
Camden
Elite Seven Books:
Gluttony
Greed

Not Safe for Zon Books:
The Wild
Hale
Bad Bad Bad
This is War, Baby
Like Dragonflies

The Breaking the Rules Series:
Broken (Book 1)
Wrong (Book 2)
Scarred (Book 3)
Mistake (Book 4)
Crushed (Book 5 – a novella)

The Vegas Aces Series:
Rock Country (Book 1)
Rock Heart (Book 2)
Rock Bottom (Book 3)

The Becoming Her Series:
Becoming Lady Thomas (Book 1)
Becoming Countess Dumont (Book 2)
Becoming Mrs. Benedict (Book 3)

Alpha & Omega Duet:
Alpha & Omega (Book 1)
Omega & Love (Book 2)

books by
NIKKI ASH

All books can be read as standalones

The Fighting Series
Fighting for a Second Chance (Secret baby)
Fighting with Faith (Secret baby)
Fighting for Your Touch
Fighting for Your Love (Single mom)
Fighting 'round the Christmas Tree: A Fighting Series Novel

Fighting Love Series
Tapping Out (Secret baby)
Clinched (Single dad)
Takedown (Single mom)

Imperfect Love Series
The Pickup (Secret baby)
Going Deep (Enemies to Lovers)
On the Surface (Second chance, single dad)

Stand-alone Novels

Bordello (Mob romance)
Knocked Down (Single dad)
Unbroken Promises (Friends to lovers)
Through His Eyes (Single mom, age gap)
Clutch Player

Co-written novels

Heath (Modern telling)
Hidden Truths
Stolen Lies

Made in the USA
Columbia, SC
28 July 2021